SNAKE CHARMER

Lynne Sella

WingSpan Press

Published in the United States and the United Kingdom by WingSpan Press, Livermore, CA

The WingSpan name, logo and colophon are the trademarks of WingSpan Publishing.

ISBN 978-1-59594-538-9

First edition 2014

Printed in the United States of America

www.wingspanpress.com

Library of Congress Control Number 2014945663

1 2 3 4 5 6 7 8 9 10

This book is dedicated to Linda Meadows,
a dear friend and fellow tap dancer,
who was tragically taken too soon from this world.

She will surely be missed by friends and family alike.

Acknowledgments

First and foremost I would like to thank my readers for patiently waiting for this second book in the Deputy Sarah Murdock series and encouraging me to finish it by constantly asking, "When is the next one going to be done?" I would also like to thank Tara and Scott Boucher, past owners of Grand View Alpaca in Janesville for allowing me to tour their ranch and learn about alpacas. I would also like to thank Australia Zoo and Las Vegas Zoo for their information on anacondas. Special thanks to Chip Jackson for his continued advice and consultation on policies and procedures of the Sheriff's Department and to fellow writers Candace Toft and Michielle Noonberg for their support and willingness to read chapter after chapter and offer suggestions on how to make it better.

SNAKE CHARMER

Chapter 1

Pete was right. The band wasn't great, but it was loud. Pete Yarbrough, owner and bartender of the Silver Spur Saloon, was the bass player for the local band that played at his bar on Friday and Saturday nights. Not that they wouldn't play anywhere else — they just hadn't been asked.

I checked my watch. *Where is she?* Cindy Evans, dispatcher for the Modoc County Sheriff's Office where I worked as a deputy, was supposed to meet me at six o'clock; it was now half-past. I wasn't sure just how much more of the band's music I could take, but I owed her a favor. Not only did she find me a place to stay at her uncle's motel when I came back to California, she'd also hauled all my stuff from Alturas to my new home in Fort Bidwell while I drove my horse cross-country from Virginia.

"Sorry I'm late." Cindy climbed up onto the bar-stool beside me. "A call came into the office just as I was getting ready to leave and my replacement was in the john." The sides of her light brown hair were pulled up, creating a cascade of curls down her back, so unlike my own hair — straight as an arrow and worn in a long, single braid. "So which one is he?"

"The bass player."

"Ooh, he looks as dreamy as he sounds." She

was right. Pete had exchanged his two-tone bowling shirt for a tight black T-shirt, which hugged his torso in all the right places. His usual five o'clock shadow was gone, making his mustache and Elvis-style sideburns stand out even more.

I hid a smile behind my beer bottle. Cindy spoke with him on the phone during my last investigation and had insisted on meeting him. Being related to half the single men in the county and not part of the date-your-cousin scene, she was definitely on a manhunt.

"I need to use the bathroom. Order me a beer, and you can introduce us when I come out." She hopped off the barstool and disappeared into the small restroom.

The band was winding down its rendition of "Takin' Care of Business" when a scream permeated the bar loud enough to be heard over the music. Silence followed as everyone looked around, uncertain as to its origin. That is, until it repeated.

"Saarrraaaahhh!!!!"

Cindy!

I leapt from my stool and tore toward the door. "Cindy," I called. "Are you all right?"

"No! Get in here!"

I grabbed the knob but it wouldn't budge. "Unlock the door."

"I can't! Oh, help me!"

Turning around, I was surprised to see Pete standing right behind me, a wad of keys in one hand and a baseball bat in the other. "It's one of these, but I'm not sure which one. Here, hold this," he said, thrusting the bat at me.

I stepped aside and let him try keys until one of

them worked and the door opened. I took a step inside and immediately knew why Cindy had screamed. A rattlesnake was curled up at the base of the toilet. Cindy, still sitting on the seat, had swung her legs around and braced her feet against the sink.

"Don't you dare laugh!" she hissed.

Instinctively I reached for my gun, but being dressed in street clothes, I wasn't wearing it.

"So, what's all the commotion?" Pete asked, poking his head around the door.

"Aaaa!! Get out! Get out!" Cindy attempted to hide behind her hands.

"It's a rattlesnake! Grab a shovel or something to kill it!" I said, trying to shove him out of the small room.

"No need for that." He pushed past me, "I'll just grab it and take it outside."

"Grab it?" Cindy and I exclaimed in unison.

"Sure. Hand me Slugger." He held out his hand, and I passed him the bat with its name tattooed on its shaft. Pete gently prodded the snake from its coiled position. Then he reached down, grasped it just above the tail and stood, dangling the reptile like a short rope. "Isn't it a beauty?" he said, holding the snake up and admiring it.

"No!" we chorused and I began backing through the doorway with my arms spread when a mountain of a man stepped up behind me.

"You need a hand, Deputy?" Hank Henrickson was a local rancher who had helped me recover a dead body several weeks earlier.

"Don't think so," I replied. "Pete's coming out with a..."

"Snake!" the huge man shrieked, backpedaling

as fast as he could. I had no idea a man his size could move so quickly, and as soon as the other patrons realized what Pete was packing, they too stepped way back.

Within seconds Cindy came out, her clothes back where they belonged, and headed for the door.

"Where are you going?" I called, chasing after her.

"Away from here. I hate snakes! I hate it when people pick up snakes, and..." she paused, "...he saw me sitting on the..." She shook her head. "He's all yours; I'm going home." She shoved open the heavy wooden door, practically knocking Pete down as he came back in, and hurried to her car.

"Your friend leaving? The snake's gone."

"Yeah, she's not feeling well." I moved back over to the bar and reclaimed my stool. Pete followed and sat next to me. "So, where'd you learn to pick up a snake like that?" I asked.

"Oh, I've been handling snakes since I was a kid."

"Didn't your parents ever tell you not to play with poisonous reptiles?"

"Uh, not really."

I gave him that you've-got-to-be-kidding-me look.

He chuckled. "My dad's a snake handler for the Pentecostal Church back in Kentucky, where I grew up."

"Oh, I see." But I didn't. *Who in their right mind plays around with poisonous snakes?*

"What'd you think about our music?" he asked.

"Not bad. What's the name of the band?"

Pete grinned, and his crystal-blue eyes sparkled. "Don't really have one. Didn't see a need for a name since we just play for fun."

"Hey Pete, you ready for another set?" one of the

band members called from the tiny stage along the south wall.

"Sure thing. Hang on a sec." He slid from the bar stool and turned to me. "You gonna stick around for a while?"

I checked my watch; it wasn't even eight o'clock yet, but I was beat and my head was beginning to throb. "If you don't mind, I think I'll take a rain check and just go on home. Had kind of a rough week, if you know what I mean." I rubbed a lump on the back of my head.

He nodded. "No problemo. Come back any time."

As he headed back toward the others, I slipped out the front door and into the cool night air. Walking to my Ford Dooley, I noticed a vintage Harley in the spot where Pete usually parked his '67 Pontiac GTO. The black and gold paint shone under the glare of the yard light, and the black leather seat begged to be straddled. While I waited for the diesel engine to warm up, I imagined what it would be like to cruise along, feeling the vibration of the motor, the wind in my hair, the — *Whoa there! Better get a grip!*

Slamming the truck into reverse, I backed away from the Silver Spur and headed north for home and a long soak in my custom-built hot tub. More of a pit lined with river rocks cemented together, the original owner had built a bathhouse over it and used a nearby hot spring to fill it. The tub had been a major selling point for the house and a luxury I indulged in often.

At the intersection of Surprise Valley Road and County Road 224, I stopped at the bank of mailboxes and opened mine. In addition to an advertisement for local hardware store and the phone bill, I found a key belonging to one of the parcel lockers. Inside was a small package from my sister, Alexis. A buyer for Nordstrom's and consummate urbanite, I couldn't imagine what she'd be sending me and hoped it wasn't a pair of slippers. Her recent visit, while interesting, had ended in disaster. I tossed the box into the cab of my truck and climbed in. Within minutes, I was rumbling down my own driveway, the throb in my head intensifying, and I made a mental note to take something as soon as I got inside.

I let myself in the door and placed the small package next to the computer on my desk as I passed through the front porch. More of a sunroom, I had converted it to an office when I moved in. After filling the kettle and placing it on the stove, I headed for the medicine cabinet in the bathroom.

By the time the water in the kettle was hot, I'd changed into my favorite Green Bay Packers T-shirt and a pair of sweats, downed three ibuprofen, and was sitting at the kitchen table, the package from Alexis before me. It was fairly heavy and made a strange clunking sound, but I opened it anyway. Inside were several bottles, some jars, and a couple of tubes. I pulled them out one by one, reading the labels as I did. Skin toners, acne creams, mudpacks, masks, and peels. The last thing to come out was a note.

Sarah darling,
   The store got in this latest line of skin care products and I immediately thought of you. Let me know if they take care of your acne problem.
   All my love,
   Alexis

Lynne Sella

Acne problem? What acne problem! I stomped into the bathroom and peered into the mirror over the sink, searching for any kind of blemish. Sure I'd had some nasty pimples before, but that was a long time ago back in high school. As I moved closer to the mirror, I could see one or two small bumps that may or may not be the beginnings of a pimple, but what really got my attention were the wrinkles around my mouth and the corners of my eyes. And when did I get the huge creases between my eyebrows!

I rushed back out to the kitchen and began reading the labels again. "...tightens skin...removes wrinkles...gives your skin that youthful look..." I grabbed up the products I thought would work best and hurried back to the bathroom. After using an apricot scrub, opening my pores with a hot washcloth, and applying a rejuvenating mask, I fixed myself a cup of tea and settled on the couch to wait the recommended fifteen minutes. As I closed my eyes and lay back, the pounding in my head subsided and I began to relax.

Chapter 2

The faint chirp of my cell phone slowly pulled me from the darkness of sleep. Semi-conscious, I struggled to my feet and stumbled toward the bedroom, stubbing my toe on the end of the couch as I went by. Hopping on one foot and cursing like a sailor, I located my pants, fished out my phone, and connected. "Murdock." Too late! Within seconds, my landline began to ring. I crawled across the bed and plucked the cordless from its cradle. "Hello?"

"Sarah, it's Cindy. I've got a call for you."

"Why are *you* contacting me? You already worked your shift."

"Ira Fielding was supposed to work, but apparently he ate something that didn't agree with him. Spent more time in the john than at the desk, so I came back in."

"Listen, I'm really sorry about tonight."

"Forget it. Seems it turned out for the best. I'm not really interested in a guy that has kids, especially little ones."

"Kids? Cindy, what are you talking about?"

"Pete. That's why I called. He just reported his baby is missing, though I can't imagine why he'd have his kid at the bar. Anyway, he needs you at the Silver Spur ay-sap."

"Yeah, okay. Call him back and let him know I'm on my way." I disconnected and slipped out of my sweats. *Pete has a child?* As I wiggled back into my jeans, I wondered how I could have missed that one.

Securing my gun belt around my waist, I stopped in my sunroom office long enough to grab my uniform jacket and stomp into my work boots. It wasn't exactly regulation, but it would do.

Thirty minutes later, I eased my patrol unit off the road and parked in front of the Silver Spur Saloon. Pete was leaning against the light pole, his arms folded across his chest. As soon as he spotted my rig, he hustled over.

"Hi Pete," I called as I opened my door and stepped out.

"Hey Sarah, I'm sure glad — Aaaaaa!" He skidded to a stop. "What have you done to yourself?" he cried, pointing at my face.

I leaned toward the Ford Explorer and looked into the side view mirror. The rejuvenating mask I'd applied earlier and promptly forgotten had hardened and turned a ghostly white, making me look like a participant in Mexico's Day of the Dead. *Unbelievable! Alexis has done it to me again!* I moved to the back of the vehicle, yanked open the rear door, and began looking for something, anything, to clean my face. Spotting a box of tissues, I pulled out a handful and attempted to remove the dried mask, but without moisture of some kind, it was not coming off. Continuing my search, I located a half-used tube of Armorall wipes. Extracting two, I tore them off and removed what I could of the hardened residue. Slightly more presentable, I slammed the door shut and went back to where Pete was waiting. "Now Pete, what's this about your child missing?"

"Not my child — my baby!" Pete walked over to where I'd seen the motorcycle. "The '69 Harley I rebuilt is gone! Stolen! Who would've taken my bike? Everyone knew it was mine!"

"Take it easy, Pete. Maybe somebody's just playing a joke on you. A very bad joke. Did you look around to see if it just got moved?"

"It's gone I tell you. You can see the boot tracks coming up to where it was parked and then the tire marks where the son-of-a-bitch drove it off!" He was right, and I hadn't even noticed until he pointed it out.

"How hard is it to hotwire a Harley? Maybe someone saw him doing it?"

Pete shook his head and his eyes glistened in the glow of the yard light. I half-expected him to break down and start bawling. "The key was in it. The goddam key was it the ignition." He threw his hands into the air. "Nobody steals in Surprise Valley."

"Did you notice anyone out of the ordinary? Someone you didn't know?"

"Friend of mine was tending bar since I was playing, but I can't get hold of her."

"You don't have her number?"

"Yeah, I got her number in my cell phone but..."

"But what?"

"My cell phone was on the bike. I forgot to take it out of the leather pouch strapped to the bitch — uh, I mean sissy bar." He wiped his nose on the back of his hand.

Reaching for my notebook, I realized I hadn't

grabbed it. "Hold on, let me get something to write on." I moved back to my rig and pulled a backup notebook out of the glove compartment. "Now," I said, returning to where Pete was waiting, "give me a description of the bike and I'll get an all-points bulletin out right away."

"It's a Harley-Davidson FLH Shovelhead, black with gold trim."

"Got it. Any distinctive marks or blemishes on it?"

"Are you serious? It was the most perfect example of..." He stopped and his brows furrowed. "I almost forgot — the left side of the seat has a rough spot from when I dumped it one time. Ran into a patch of sand on a turn and it slid out from under me. Got road rash from my ankle to my ass but the only mark on the bike was that spot on the seat."

"Okay. I'll call it in, and then I'll take you home."

"Give me a minute to lock up the bar, and I'll be right there."

I climbed into the front seat and grabbed the mic of my radio. "Modoc, 113."

"Go ahead 113, this is Modoc."

"I need you to put out an APB right away."

"Don't you mean an Amber Alert?"

"Negative. The 'baby' is a '69 Harley-Davidson. Black with gold trim and a scarred spot on the driver's side of the seat."

"Oh for Pete's sake!"

"Yeah, for his sake I hope we locate it. I'll fill you in later. 113, 10-10."

"Copy 113. Time 3:05."

I'd just hung up the mic when Pete opened the

passenger door and got in. "Thanks for the lift. I really didn't want to hoof it home."

"All in a day's work." I started the engine and headed south. A few minutes later I turned onto Laxaque Road. Traveling another quarter of a mile, I drove down a familiar, narrow driveway. "Gee, the last time I was here, a rock bounced off my windshield."

"That's right. You hauled Bill off the night he was chucking rocks at my windows. Looks like I owe you twice. How about I make you breakfast?"

"Oh, you don't have to do that." I pulled alongside the small trailer.

"It's no big deal. Make it every day after I close the bar. It's a secret recipe I got from Shellie — supposed to ward off hangovers."

"Shellie?"

"She's the friend who covers for me when the band plays. She was there tonight."

He was right. Someone else had served my beer, but I hadn't really noticed who it was.

"Anyway, she swears by it — scrambled eggs with pesto, onions, and asiago cheese." He opened the passenger door. "Come on in and I'll whip us up a batch."

I checked the digital clock on the dash. It was already half-past three; I was hungry, and sleeping in was definitely in my future. "All right," I said, shutting off the engine, "but I get to help."

"Deal."

Chapter 3

As soon as I woke up, I knew something was wrong. I bounded out of bed, ran for the bathroom and peered into the mirror. My face felt as though it was on fire and looked like it had a bad case of diaper rash. The skin under my eyes was puffed up like a marshmallow, and I doubted my own mother would have recognized me. *Probably should have washed my face when I got home.* I lathered up a washcloth with a bar of Ivory soap and gently cleaned my face. Then I rinsed the cloth in cool water and held it against my irritated skin, temporarily soothing the burning sensation. Lowering the cloth, I peered into the mirror again. No change. *Great!*

I grabbed the small white wastebasket, stomped into the kitchen, and swept all the skin care products I'd left scattered across the table into it. Only feeling slightly satisfied, I filled the coffee maker with water, scooped some Folgers into the basket, and waited.

When the pot was only half full, I poured myself a huge mug, walked through the house and made a mental note of all the chores I'd neglected during my last investigation involving a dead body in possession of Indian artifacts and a double homicide. If it hadn't been for Remy, my nosy neighbor and self-appointed partner, I would've been listed among the casualties, too. But everything turned out all right and now my biggest concern was getting caught up.

After changing into a pair of faded jeans and an old T-shirt, I rounded up all the dirty laundry, and while it went through the wash cycle, I dusted and vacuumed, mopped the floors and cleaned the bathroom, avoiding my reflection in the mirror as much as possible. Then I moved the wet clothes from the washer to the dryer and headed for the barn.

As I trudged down the driveway, Raven approached the gate and greeted me with a gleeful whinny and a toss of his head. "And good morning to you, big fella," I said, pausing long enough to rub his huge, flat forehead. "How are you today?" The black gelding I'd come to think of as a close friend whinnied again, arched his back and crowhopped before trotting across the grassy pasture, his black mane and tail trailing behind him. I was tempted to throw the saddle on him and explore the mountain behind my house but cleaning the water trough and mucking out the stall were on the agenda instead. As I reached into the algae-infested, antique bathtub and pulled out the slime-slick plug, I promised myself the next day would be devoted to equine pleasure.

Leaving the tub to drain, I retrieved a rake, shovel, and wheelbarrow from the small tack room and got started on Raven's stall. Being allowed to come and go as he pleased, the gelding had not spent much time in there, so it only took three trips to the manure pile to finish the job. By then the tub-turned-trough was empty, so I scrubbed it down with a bristle brush and rinsed it out with the hose. Then I replaced the plug, tossed the hose inside to refill it, and moved on to do the same to the hot tub.

A few minutes later, I emerged from the bathhouse, my clothes as wet from the inside as they were from the outside. Sweat ran down my face in rivulets and wiping it off on the short sleeve of my T-shirt was pure agony. Heading back to the barn to put away the bristle brush, I was stunned to find Raven standing over the water trough, the hose dangling from his mouth.

"Raven, drop that!" I shouted as I hurried toward him. Disobedient as a toddler, he tossed his head. But in doing so, he caused the water coming out of the end of the hose to hit his rump. That made him kick up his back feet and toss his head. Again the water hit his rump, and he shifted his weight to his back legs and spun.

"Whoa, Raven! Whoa!" I sprinted toward the gate, afraid he'd tangle himself in the hose. Instead, he tossed his head one more time, releasing the hose as he did. It went flying and so did the horse toward the far end of the pasture. I returned the hose to the trough and the bristle brush to the tack room, and then went back to the house. I had to find something to soothe the skin on my face.

A thorough search of my bathroom yielded nothing for a rash and the only moisturizer I had was a small bottle of peppermint-scented foot cream. Desperate, I jammed my sunglasses onto my face, grabbed my keys, and headed out the door.

"Remy," I called as I rounded the side of his double-wide. *Must be here somewhere.* I'd parked next to his early model Toyota Land Cruiser. Still recovering from a recent head injury, I was concerned when he didn't respond to my knocking. That is until I heard hammering coming from the back of the house. "Remy," I called again when there was a pause in the pounding.

"Back here." His speech seemed distorted, and the instant I spotted him, I knew why. Nails dangled from his mouth as he attempted to attach wire to the post of some large pen.

"What are you building?" I asked, moving in next to him and holding the wire in place.

"Repairing the deer fence for my garden." He finished pounding in the nail he'd been working on. "It's the only way to keep 'em out of my melons and tomatoes." He removed the large, black felt hat from his head and mopped his brow with the handkerchief from his back pocket, leaving droplets of sweat in his white beard and moustache. His green plaid shirt was open over a white T-shirt and his faded jeans just touched the laces of his brown work boots. "So what brings you by?" he asked, replacing the hat and the handkerchief.

"I have a problem I was hoping you could help me with."

"Be glad to. Ain't that what partners are for?" He started toward the small porch that ran along the back of his place. "Come on up here and set a spell." Reluctantly, I followed him and settled into one of his old metal lawn chairs. "Now, what can I do to help?" he asked.

I removed my sunglasses and pushed my hair away from my face. "Well..." I began.

"What in tarnation happened to you? Looks like you fell face first into a patch of poison oak."

Keeping the story brief, I explained what had happened and asked Remy if he had anything that might give me some relief.

"You know, I believe I do." He heaved himself out of his chair. "Come on inside, and I'll see if I can find it." He led the way through the back door and into the kitchen. "Have a seat," he said, pointing to my usual spot at the small wooden table covered with a red and white checkered tablecloth, "and I'll be right back."

Looking around, I was certain the kitchen hadn't changed much since Remy's wife, Peggy, had passed. Her hankering — as he put it — for roosters was evident in the canisters, trivets, and towels that decorated the room. One addition I knew of was the "newfangled contraption" he'd bought to make fresh-baked bread.

"Found it," he called, slamming a cupboard door. He came back into the kitchen, carrying two different shaped bottles. "This here witch hazel should cool your skin." He set the taller of the two on the table. "And this will help with the itch." The other bottle was half-full of a light pink liquid.

"I haven't used calamine lotion since I was a kid. I didn't know they still made it."

"Not sure they do. I've had that there bottle for quite a spell but it should still be good."

I thanked Remy and drove back to my place, anxious to stop the incessant itching and spend the rest of the day relaxing. I was not, however, prepared for what I found.

A white panel van was parked next to the house, and it wasn't until I pulled up next to it that I could see "Pet Express" painted down its side along with the silhouette of a Scottish terrier.

Snake Charmer

"What the..." I climbed out of my Ford Dooley and approached the driver, who was standing on my front steps. "Can I help you?"

"Sarah Murdock?" The guy had on the typical deliveryman attire; dark shorts, light shirt, ball cap with the company logo on it, and secret-agent style sunglasses.

"Yes," I said tentatively.

"Got a delivery for you, if you'd step this way."

"There must be some mistake. I haven't ordered anything." I followed him to the double doors at the back of the van and watched him unload a small dog carrier and two pieces of luggage; red, with small black paw prints. *Can't be!* "Where did these come from? Who sent them?"

"It's all explained in here." Larry, or at least that was the name on his shirt, pulled an envelope off his clipboard and handed it to me. "Sign here, line seven."

I held up both hands and stepped back. "I said there must be a mistake."

"Look lady, I don't have time for this." He tucked the clipboard under one arm and slammed the doors shut. "I'm due back in the bay area by six o'clock tonight, and I'm going to be late as it is. I've made my delivery of one..." He glanced at his paperwork. "Shorkie, so if you don't mind, sign on line seven and let me get on the road." He shoved the clipboard and pen at me.

Not knowing what else to do, I signed on line seven and watched Larry get into his van, make a three-point turn, and drive away. *Alexis strikes again!*

Grabbing the stuff I'd gotten from Remy, I left my

recent delivery in the driveway while I went inside to treat my rash. Using a handful of toilet paper, I dabbed the witch hazel all over my face and felt instant cooling relief. Then I applied the calamine lotion to the worse spots, which pretty much ended up being my whole face. I looked like a pink geisha, but the itching was gone. Feeling better, I went outside, gathered up my sister's dog and its accessories, and came back inside to read the letter.

> My dearest Sarah,
> I did it! I got the promotion and I am flying to Paris in the morning. Because I must be gone for almost a month, I need someone to look after Bubbles, and you were the first person I thought of. The two of you got along so well during my last visit, I just knew you wouldn't mind, and I couldn't leave her with Sterling because he's coming with me as my photographer. It's the perfect opportunity for him as well, and we'll get to see the most romantic city in the world together.
> Please take good care of my baby and I'll see you soon.
> All my love,
> Alexis
>
> P.S. I didn't have time to pack up her favorite food but any gourmet brand will do.
> P.P.S. Keep her away from that nasty neighbor of yours. I don't think he likes Bubbles.

A month! I didn't want to put up with her dust mop of a mutt for one day. Peering into the dog carrier I'd set on the coffee table, I wasn't surprised to find Bubbles dressed in a pink camo jacket and matching ball cap, complete with ear holes. *Good grief!*

The dog clothes reminded me that Alexis had claimed our mother had purchased most of them. Why hadn't she sent Bubbles to live with her? But I knew why. According to my dad, a dog — a real dog — has to weigh at least fifty pounds and take up most of a large dog bed. If it didn't, the animal was nothing but an obnoxious, damn nuisance. And Bubbles definitely fit in that category.

Wondering what other canine fashions my sister had sent, I popped open the larger piece of luggage, which resembled an old-fashioned steamer trunk. One side held a variety of outfits — some I recognized from the previous visit — each one on its own tiny hanger. The other side had three small drawers. The top one held a variety of bows, jeweled clips and collars, and a miniature tiara. The middle drawer contained footwear ranging from tennis shoes to cowboy boots to patent leather mary janes. A pink satin robe with matching bunny slippers, several hats, and a pair of strap-on sunglasses were crammed into the bottom one. *The dog has a better wardrobe than I do!*

I didn't open the other piece of luggage because I already knew it held portable dog dishes trimmed with rhinestones. Alexis had filled it with gourmet dog food and bottled water when she was here, but that wouldn't be happening this time!

Scooting the carrier closer, I pinched the latch and pulled the door open. The tiny blond dog stepped out onto the table, her nails clicking against the surface and sat down in front of me. "Well dog, looks like we're stuck with each other for a while." Taking another look at the ridiculous outfits, I remembered I had my own laundry to fold and put away.

As I headed for the back door, I heard Bubbles leap down from the table and follow me out to the pump house that doubled as a laundry room. She seemed to enjoy herself exploring the backyard as I tugged things out of the dryer and into the clothes basket. "Come on Bubbles," I called as I headed back into the house, but the pink camo-clad canine ignored me and continued her exploration. I considered what to do — for about five seconds — and then went back into the house.

I'd put away all the clean clothes and scrounged a couple of empty whipped topping bowls out of a drawer in the kitchen before I heard scratching at the back door. Not sure whether I was disappointed or relieved, I let the dog in and showed her where I'd placed her new dog dishes. She had a few laps of water, sniffed the empty one and looked up at me.

"Guess I'll have to get you some food when I go into Cedarville tomorrow." I opened the fridge and found a small piece of cheese and some meatloaf Remy had sent home the last time we had dinner together. "Here, this will have to do for now," I said, dropping the food into the bowl.

Bubbles gave it a sniff, lay down next to the bowl, and rested her head on her outstretched paws. I got the message loud and clear but figured the dog would rethink her decision if she got hungry enough.

I'd gone back into the living room to tidy up when my cell phone rang. I flipped it open and answered. "Hello."

"Murdock?"

I thought I recognized the voice but couldn't place it. "Yeah?"

"Just got a call from a rancher in Eagleville. Something about a missing animal. Says it can't wait but since I don't want to pull a deputy off patrol over here, I figured I'd send you."

"Undersheriff Sandusky?"

"That's right."

"What are you doing at dispatch?"

"Fielding is still out with food poisoning and no one else was available. Rancher's name is Robertson and the address is 14771 County Road 1. Should be on the right, just before the cemetery. Get out there as soon as possible." Then he hung up.

Dirk Sandusky, or Dirk the Jerk as some of the deputies called him, was a real pain in the ass. Not only did he lack respect for female officers, he despised me for being a former FBI agent. Unable to pass the psychological evaluation, his own application to the Bureau had been denied. That, combined with not following procedure on the Gus Miller case and contacting the FBI after he told me not to, made it almost impossible to work with the man. But since the sheriff was out of town at the National Sheriffs' Association conference, I had no choice but to do what Sandusky said.

Since this wasn't an actual emergency, I took the time to put on my uniform and braid my hair. But when I looked into the mirror, I realized I needed something to hide my hideous face. My sunglasses helped some, but I needed more. Grabbing my ball cap with the sheriff's logo on it, I pulled it down over my glasses as far as I could. *Not perfect, but it'll do.*

A few minutes later I was in my patrol unit headed for Eagleville, which was forty-five minutes away. *So much for my relaxing afternoon.*

Chapter 4

I had just driven through Cedarville when I remembered I'd left Bubbles in the house alone. Not that I was worried about her being by herself but because I recalled something my sister had said about the dog chewing up things. All I could do was hope the damn mutt was still pouting next to the dog dish.

The ranch was easy to find and so was the rancher. Dressed in wranglers, a short-sleeve cotton shirt and John Deere ball cap, he was standing in front of his house, arms folded across his chest. "Mr. Robertson?" I asked when I approached.

"That's right. Bob Robertson." He stared at me for several seconds, took off his cap and scratched his head. After replacing the cap he continued. "I've been waiting for some time."

"Sorry about that. I had to come from Fort Bidwell." I took out my notebook. "You reported a missing animal?"

"One of my alpacas."

"And when did you discover it was missing?"

"Around noon. I was checking the fence line and realized it was gone."

"From this field?" I asked, pointing to my left.

Approximately eight animals, each one solid black or brown in color, were peacefully grazing.

"No, those are the adult males." Bob moved toward a larger field, which was located behind the house and adjacent to a state-of-the-art barn, which looked more like a warehouse than an outbuilding. "The females and youngsters are back here." Like the males, the females were mostly solid black or brown, but at least two of them were white. "Yesterday I had two white crias, but as you can see I only have one now."

"Crias?"

"Baby alpacas."

"Oh. And you're sure it didn't get through the fence?"

He shook his head. "Not these. No-climb fencing plus a hot wire running across the top keeps my alpacas in and other animals out. Besides, I check it every day. These here animals are worth quite a chunk of change, so I can't take a chance on one of them wandering off."

The grass in the field was too short to hide anything bigger than a cottontail rabbit. At the far end I noticed an area of larger vegetation. "What about over there?"

"Nope. I searched all around that pond. Not so much as a white hair."

"Is it possible someone carried it off?"

"Don't see how, not with the LGD in the field."

"LGD?"

"Livestock Guardian Dog." He nodded toward the far left corner of the field where a large dog perched on its haunches, reminding me of a sheep dog on an old cartoon I'd watched as a kid.

"What is that? A golden lab?"

"Anatolian Shepherd. Ol' Champ don't tolerate no strangers, man or beast. Any come around and he starts barking."

"But you didn't hear him last night or this morning?"

"Not a peep. Had no idea anything was wrong until I noticed the missing cria."

"Well if you don't mind, I'd like to do some investigating," I said as I moved back toward the Ford Explorer. "Then I'll fill out the crime report. Do you have a picture or registration information to help identify the animal?"

"Sure do. I'll get it while you look around." Leaving me to do my job, Mr. Robertson disappeared inside the house.

I slipped my notebook into my pocket and dug the digital camera out of my evidence case in the back of my unit. Then I walked past the house toward the barn and through a small gate. As soon as I latched it behind me, I had the full attention of twenty camelids and one canine.

Strolling down the fence line, the first thing I noticed was the lack of bare soil on either side of the wire fencing. *So much for locating shoe prints.* The second thing I noticed was a very large dog heading my way.

Champ got within twenty feet of me, his nose in the air, and raised the alarm. The first bark was so loud and incredibly deep, I'm sure I jumped several inches. And no amount of coaxing or cooing on my part convinced him to stop.

"Champ, here!" It was the rancher. "Here, boy!" The dog ceased his barking and sniffed the air one last time before trotting over to his master.

Continuing my inspection of the perimeter, I found nothing out of the ordinary until I reached the pond. Located in the upper right corner of the field, it was about thirty feet long and fifteen feet across, and a clump of willows grew between it and the fence. As I pushed past the branches, I noticed the corner post was sturdier than the others and reinforced by what looked like a modified railroad tie set at an angle from the top of the post to the ground, which a more agile individual might use to get over the fence. Moving closer, I checked for shoe prints or trampled grass. Nothing.

The pond itself had some kind of vegetation, possibly water lilies, filling most of it, and a small outlet passed under the fence through a shallow channel. And unless a baby alpaca can flatten itself to the ground, crawl on its belly, and squeeze through an opening smaller than it is, the animal didn't get out that way. But something had happened to it.

As I inspected the remaining section of fence, I surveyed the surrounding acreage and found no significant foliage for nearly a quarter of a mile in any direction. No place a baby alpaca could conceal itself.

"Find anything?" Mr. Robertson called as I got closer. He was leaning against the gate, his arms once more folded across his chest.

I shook my head. "Nothing. Did you poke around in the pond, under that vegetation?"

"No need to. It's fed by a hot spring, so the alpacas don't tend to wade into it, and it's only a couple feet deep." He held out some papers as he swung the gate open for me. "Scanned you a copy of the registration and a picture."

"Thanks. This will help when I fill out the report." I dug out one of my cards and handed it to him. "Give me a call if you have any more trouble, and I'll watch for the animal as I patrol the valley."

Opening the front door of my house, my worst fears were realized when I heard growling and the sound of tearing fabric. I dropped the bag of dog food and six-pack of beer I'd bought on the way home and rushed into the living room. The dog, its front paws firmly planted on one end of a piece of material, had the other end in her mouth and was shaking her head from side to side.

"Bubbles, stop that!" I yelled. Dashing across the room, I snatched up the demonic dog and held her at arm's length for almost a full minute before she calmed down and dropped the cloth. Still holding the mutt, I looked around the room.

The trunk that held the dog clothes was lying open on the floor, its edges decorated with teeth marks. The drawers had also been gnawed, their contents torn and scattered. The only item of canine clothing still in one piece was a single cowboy boot. I placed Bubbles on the sofa and began gathering up the wreckage. The dog watched me for a few seconds and then lay down, her head on her paws. When I had everything back in the luggage, I took both pieces and shoved them in the closet of the back bedroom. Bubbles was still on the sofa when I passed through on the way to the kitchen.

I tore open the bag of dog food and poured some into her bowl, covering what I'd put in there earlier. Pulling the rest of Remy's leftovers out of the fridge, I popped them into the microwave, grabbed a beer, and sat at the table. As I waited for my food to get warm, my four-legged guest trotted into the kitchen, lapped up some more water and then sniffed at the dog food. Placing her tiny front paw on the edge of the dish, she tipped the plastic white bowl until most of it dumped out onto the floor, exposing the cheese and meatloaf, which she gobbled down.

Completely baffled, I carried my own dinner into the living room, settled onto the sofa, and turned on the television. Before too long Bubbles joined me, and we fell asleep watching a *MacGyver* rerun.

Chapter 5

Sometime during the night, I must've stumbled to bed because I woke the next morning to find myself face-to-face with a small blond dog. Not only had she climbed onto my bed, she made herself comfortable on my favorite pillow.

"Really, dog?" I said as I rolled out of bed and hurried to the bathroom. After a quick shower, I reluctantly looked at my face in the mirror and was surprised to see most of the redness was gone. I dabbed more witch hazel on it, secured my hair in its usual braid, and went back into the bedroom.

Bubbles had vacated her spot, so I made the bed, pulled on a clean pair of jeans and a long-sleeved shirt, and headed for the kitchen. A simple breakfast of eggs and toast with a cup of instant coffee, I was ready to spend the day with Raven. I escorted my sister's dog outside on my way to the barn; she immediately resumed her exploration of the property, and I never gave her a second thought.

The large, black gelding greeted me at the gate and began nudging me with his velvety nose. "What?" I asked, petting his flat forehead. "You think I have something for you?" Taking advantage of his curiosity, I grabbed his halter from the tack room and slipped it into place before relinquishing the apple I'd tucked into my pocket. Secured to the hitching post with a lead rope, Raven stood head lowered and eyes closed while I groomed him. That is, until Bubbles trotted between his front legs.

His head came up, pulling against the rope, and his nostrils flared. He scrambled from side to side, as if on tiptoe. He reminded me of an elephant trying to get away from a mouse, and if he could've managed it, I'm sure he would have climbed onto the hitching post and balanced there until the miniature furry monster that had attacked him was gone.

"Whoa fellow," I said, grabbing his halter and petting his massive neck. "Take it easy. I've got you." Without loosening my grip on Raven's halter, I located the walking dust mop, who'd been oblivious to the commotion, and gently launched her with my foot away from the panicked animal. "No Bubbles. Sit. Stay." To my amazement, she dropped her lower half to the ground and waited. I quickly finished grooming the horse and left him tied to the hitching post, so I could gather the few supplies I'd need on my ride.

"Come on, Dog," I said, slapping the side of my leg a few times. "There's no way you're staying down here." She immediately got up and followed me back to the house. Sitting in the middle of the kitchen floor, she watched as I threw together a couple of sandwiches, grabbed some bottled water, and changed into my riding boots.

"Now," I said, turning my attention to her, "what am I going to do with you while I'm gone?" The first thing I thought of was the small carrier she came in, but looking at it again I decided it was too confining.

Leaving her unattended in the house was out of the question, and I didn't want to lock her in the small shed out back. Then I remembered how Alexis had carried the dog around in those giant handbags of hers. "I think I have an idea," I said to Bubbles.

I tossed my supplies into a plastic grocery bag, and we returned to the barn. After placing my endurance saddle on Raven's back and cinching it tight, I threw the nylon saddlebags on behind and tied them down. Then I stuffed the snacks into one side and Bubbles into the other, leaving the opening large enough for her to poke her head through but small enough to prevent her from jumping out. Last thing, I slipped Raven's bridle into place, and we were ready to go.

Fee Reservoir is eight miles east of my house and was discovered while I was searching for a suspect. Its presence on a desert plateau surrounded by scraggly juniper trees gives it a surreal feeling, and I'd been looking forward to exploring the area. Apparently I wasn't the only one. As soon as I turned my horse toward the driveway, he began prancing and tossing his head as if he were leading a parade.

"Easy, boy." I reined in his head. "We have a long ride ahead of us." Controlling the big gelding was not easy, but I kept him to a walk until we passed Remy's house and reached the gravel road. Then I shifted my weight forward and gave the animal his head.

Raven snorted and quickened his step, falling into the pacer-like stride used on our endurance rides. As we sped down the road, I heard rustling and felt movement. Glancing behind me, I saw that Bubbles had managed to get her head through the opening, her tongue and ears flapping in the breeze, and I laughed out loud. If Alexis could see her precious puppy, she'd have kittens.

After the first couple of miles, Raven began to relax and so did his pace. Dropping back into a slow trot, he continued up Fee Reservoir Road toward the desert plateau. We traveled that way for almost half an hour until the road began its gentle climb. Then he slowed to a walk, his head bobbing up and down with each long stride.

As we approached the reservoir, I heard a sound like the faint drone of a mosquito. Looking to the south, I spotted a plume of alkali dust along the eastern shore of Upper Lake. "Probably a dirt bike," I announced to no one in particular.

I rode past the boat ramp and through the tiny campground, thinking it would be the perfect place to have lunch before heading home. Guiding Raven off the dirt road, we moved northeast, and I relinquished control again, letting him plot his own course through the sagebrush and junipers. Lulled by the rocking motion and the warmth of the sun beating down on my back and shoulders, I leaned back and closed my eyes. Had I not done so, I might have saved myself.

An explosion of feathers erupted from a large sagebrush nearby. Startled by the sudden flight of the damn bird, the horse leapt sideways and sent me crashing to the ground, flat on my back. Knocked breathless, I was unable to call to Raven before he disappeared over the small rise to my right. Scrambling to my feet and gasping for air, I hoped to catch him before he got too far. I ran to the top of the small knoll and was surprised at the distance he'd managed to cover. "Raven!" I stuck my fingers in my mouth and whistled, but the horse and his canine passenger kept going south toward Upper Lake. Cursing my bad luck, I trudged after them. As I watched my ride get further and further away, the unexpected ignition of a two-stroke engine drew my attention. The dirt bike rider was on the move again and heading straight for Raven. *What the hell is he doing?*

I quickened my pace but found it difficult running across the sandy soil in my riding boots. Helpless, I watched the bike catch up to Raven and then speed ahead of him. Suddenly, the rider began weaving back and forth, all the while decreasing his speed and forcing the runaway gelding from a full gallop to a brisk walk. After cutting his engine and laying the bike on its side, he jumped off, held out his hands, and waited. Amazingly, my horse walked right up to him.

Still two hundred yards away, I redoubled my effort to cover the distance but, like so many dreams I'd had as a kid, felt like I was getting nowhere. By the time I reached them, I had a stitch in my side and was gulping for air. "Thanks," I gasped, reaching out for the reins.

"I'll hold him 'til you get your wind back." Muffled by the tinted face shield of his helmet, the rider's voice sounded strangely familiar.

Nodding, I bent forward and placed my hands on my knees until my breathing slowed enough to speak. "Really appreciate you stopping him. No telling how far he would've gone."

"Glad I was here and could help." The rider handed over the reins. "How did he get away from you?"

"Damn bird in a bush spooked him."

"Don't tell me you fell off!"

Who is this guy? The skintight, blue and black pants and matching jersey, while enticing, offered no clue to his identity. "I'm sorry, do we know each other?"

The rider tugged his chinstrap loose. When he pulled off the helmet, I was greeted by crystal-blue eyes and a huge smile.

"Pete! What on earth are you doing here?"

"Might ask you the same question. I ride up this way every Sunday. The terrain is great for practicing." He stepped around me, perched his helmet on Raven's saddle, and pulled off his gloves.

"Practicing for what?"

"Motocross. Got a competition coming up in Nevada."

"Have you been riding long?"

"Ever since I was big enough to straddle a dirt bike."

"And that little trick you used to stop Raven. How did you know it would work?"

"My kid sister had a horse, and she used to fall off all the time too."

"I don't fall off all the time!" I objected.

Pete shrugged. "Anyway, I was usually the one to go after it. One day I was just screwing around and discovered I could slow the stupid animal down by weaving in front of it. It doesn't work all the time but..." He shrugged again and leaned against the saddlebags. "Aaaa!" he cried, leaping away from Raven. "There's something in there."

"Bubbles!" I'd forgotten all about the dog — again.

"No, it moved!"

35

"Relax, it's only a dog." I opened the zipper, reached inside, and held her out for Pete's inspection.

"That your dog?"

"Yes, I mean no. Not really." I slid Bubbles back into her side of the saddlebags. "It's my sister's dog, and I got shanghaied into taking care of it while she's in Paris."

"Texas?"

I rolled my eyes. "France." I plucked Pete's helmet off my saddle and handed it to him. "I've got some sandwiches if you want to follow me back to the campground." I nodded toward the reservoir.

"Got some provisions myself. It'll be like a picnic." He shoved his helmet onto his head and walked back to his bike. "Race you there," he said, his voice muffled again. He straddled his ride and fired it up.

Raven sidestepped as I tried to get on, but I managed to keep my balance long enough to swing my leg over and secure both feet in the stirrups. Then I spun the gelding around and squeezed his sides with my legs. He lunged forward, and we headed for the reservoir.

Seconds later, Pete passed me, winding his way around the intermittent sagebrush. As we approached the small rise where Raven had disappeared earlier, he increased his speed and launched himself into the air. Taking that as his cue, my horse veered right and sailed over a huge sagebrush. Fortunately, I'd been riding with my weight slightly forward, so I kept my seat and hoped Bubbles was able to do the same.

By the time I got to the campground, Pete had leaned his dirt bike against a juniper tree and was unstrapping some kind of bundle. I dismounted and looped the reins over the lower branches of a smaller tree. Then I untied the saddlebags and pulled them off, dog and all.

"Okay Mutt," I said, retrieving Bubbles and setting her on the ground. "Go sniff around and do your thing."

The tiny dog trotted toward Raven. "Hey!" She stopped and looked back at me. "Not that way. You stay away from the horse." I pointed toward the water. "Go over there." Bubbles took one more look at my horse and then trotted off toward the reservoir.

As I set out the sandwiches and water on the nearest picnic table, Pete unrolled his bundle, creating a small cloud of alkali dust. "Got a couple of sodas and some jerky, but I wouldn't mind having one of those sandwiches." He held out one of the cans. "Wanna trade?"

"Sure." I handed over one of the sandwiches, which had been intended for the dog, and swapped it for the soda.

"Just be careful when you open it because..."

Before he could finish, I popped the tab and sprayed him with most of the contents. "Oh Pete," I began, "I'm so sorry." I set the can down and looked around for something to mop up the mess.

The sticky liquid dripped from his hair and ran down in dusty rivulets. Pete untied the red bandana from around his neck and began wiping off his face.

"Here, let me help you." I took the cloth and dabbed at his hair. Then I started to wipe off the giant 'Z' on the front of his jersey.

"You don't have to do that."

"It'll just take a second." I continued to wipe off the soda.

"No really, you need to stop," he protested. He took hold of both my arms just above the elbow, and for a moment our eyes met. And then he kissed me square on the mouth, a long lingering kiss. When we parted, he flashed that big smile of his. "I warned you to stop."

"What?" It was as if my brain had stopped functioning.

"I said, I warned..."

"I heard you." I took a step back. "What was that?"

"You mean the kiss?"

I nodded. *Focus Sarah.*

Pete grinned again. "Guess it was just my way of saying thanks." He straddled one of the benches and sat down.

Is he serious? I hadn't been kissed like that since — who the hell was I kidding? I'd never been kissed like that. Watching him unwrap his sandwich, I was uncertain as to how I should feel. Angry? Embarrassed? Grateful?

Are you crazy? Go for it! I heard Sue's voice clearly, as if she were standing next to me. Sue James and I had met at Quantico and, before I left the FBI to become a deputy sheriff, she had been trying to set me up with anyone she could, no matter how much I resisted.

"Well then, you're welcome," I said, sitting across from him.

He bit off a corner of sandwich but stopped midchew. "Is peanut butter supposed to crunch?" he asked, around the mouthful.

"Apple slices." As if to show him it was safe, I took a bite of mine. "It's not pesto and eggs but..."

"Pesto and eggs!" He put down his sandwich and leaned toward me. "I saw Shellie yesterday and asked if she'd noticed anyone out of the ordinary Friday night, and she had. Some guy she'd never seen before came in about the time we started playing. What attracted her attention, I guess, was his dark aura."

"His what?"

He chuckled. "She reads people's auras."

"Interesting. She tell you what he looked like?"

"Said he looked like Rambo — long dark hair and scraggly beard. Camo pants and one of those green army jackets."

Why does that seem familiar? "Did she happen to know when he left?" Not terribly hungry, I settled for a piece of jerky and some water.

"Not exactly, but she doesn't remember seeing him after that whole snake thing." He picked up his sandwich and continued eating. When it was gone, he ate mine too and finished off his soda, which he'd opened more skillfully than I had opened mine. Then he got up and stretched. "Hate to eat and run but I really need to go." He threw the trash away, re-rolled his bundle and strapped it onto the dirt bike. "Still got some chores to do before dark and it'll take some time to get home, but before I go..." He walked back over to the table and sat backward on the bench next to me. "This was nice. Think we might repeat it sometime, I mean, maybe have dinner? I'm sure Shellie'd watch the bar for me if you're interested."

"Like a date?" I pictured Sue doing cartwheels.

"Yeah. You say when." He stood and pulled me up beside him. "Until then..." His hands caressed the sides of my face and his lips briefly touched mine. Next thing I knew, he was on his dirt bike and heading over the rise.

While the mosquito-like drone of the motorcycle faded, I gathered the remnants of the picnic and stuffed them back into the saddlebags. It wasn't until I began tying them to the back of the saddle that I remembered. "Crap, the damn dog!" Scanning the immediate area I saw no movement anywhere.

"Bubbles," I called, heading in the direction where I'd last seen the mutt. "Here, girl." Nothing. I was beginning to panic. *How am I ever going to explain this to Alexis?* Finally I spotted something running along the shoreline, but it was too far away to make a positive identification. It looked like the tiny dog I was searching for but this animal was darker, almost black in color. "Bubbles?" As it got closer, I realized it was the missing mutt, and that she had something in her mouth.

"What have you been up to?" My sister's prima donna pooch was covered in gooey mud from her nose to her tail and by the smell that wasn't all she'd rolled in. The stick in her mouth turned out to be the skeletal remains of a rabbit's hindquarter. Worst of all, when I tried to pick her up, we both yelped in pain. Some sort of prickly seed pods were entangled in the fur on her belly and the longer hair on her legs. No matter how I tried to grasp her, they poked into her tender skin as well as my hands. Eventually, I used the plastic bag from lunch to scoop her up and get her into the saddlebags.

The ride home was miserable. Bubbles cried most

of the time, obviously in pain as she bounced along in the saddlebags, and my hands began to itch and burn where the seed pods had poked me. An hour later we plodded down the driveway, anxious to be done with our excursion. In record time, I had Raven unsaddled and turned out to pasture and was carrying a very grumpy dog toward the bathhouse.

Not wanting to rinse her off in the hot tub I'd cleaned the day before, I connected a hose to the spigot and stuck it out of the window. Holding her by the scruff of the neck, I managed to spray off most of the muck. Then I wrapped her in an old towel, grabbed my electric clippers out of the tack room, and headed for the house.

Entering through the back door, I grabbed a pair of scissors as I passed through the kitchen on the way to the bathroom. I placed Bubbles in the bathtub and plugged in the shears. Being careful not to nick her skin, I cut out as many of the prickly seed pods as I could with the scissors, removing large patches of fur as well. By the time I was done, the poor dog looked like a poodle with a really bad do.

"Well Dog," I said, reaching for the shears, "I don't think we have a choice here. I just hope it grows back quickly in the next few weeks." Starting at the chest, I systematically removed the remaining clumps of fur from the underside of the dog, but when I got to the section between the hind legs, I made an astounding discovery. Two tiny testicles, previously hidden by long hair, dangled where there shouldn't be any. "You're a boy? Unbelievable!"

Chapter 6

Monday morning started out like any other work-day except I couldn't move. My back ached and my legs felt like limb wood. As I struggled to my feet, Bubbles rolled over on her back — no wait, on his back — and stretched. *Dumb dog!* A hot shower helped loosen my muscles a little, but I still hobbled around like I was a hundred years old.

Wanting to give myself some time to limber up, I decided to type up my notes from the missing cria case and print the pictures I'd taken. By the time I had the information stuck onto the blank wall of my office, which served as my evidence board, I'd upgraded from a hobble to a limp.

Dressed in my uniform with my hair secured in a long braid down my back, I was ready to start my patrol. Or at least I thought I was until Bubbles followed me to the front door, his toenails clicking against the linoleum. Once again I'd forgotten about the dog and the dilemma of what to do with him while I was gone. "Maybe Remy will keep an eye on you," I told the mutt as we headed for the Explorer.

I opened my door, and he leapt into the seat, jumped across the console, and stood with his front paws on the armrest of the passenger door. "Don't get too comfortable. You won't be here long." But I was wrong — again.

Remy's driveway was empty, his Land Cruiser nowhere in sight. "Now, where do you suppose he went?" I asked my furry copilot. But it didn't really matter because without him, I was stuck with the dog for the day. I'd just have to make the best of it and hope nothing too serious happened.

Working my way toward Cedarville, I drove up Fandango Pass Road to the summit and back. After giving Bubbles a potty break, I patrolled through Lake City and continued south on County Road 17 until it came out on the main road. Then I back-tracked a few miles, turned east, and cruised along the maze of roads between Upper and Middle Alkali Lakes, emerging onto Highway 299 near the Nevada border. As I gave Bubbles a few minutes to take care of business, my stomach growled. "Let's go, Dog. Lunchtime." Fifteen minutes later, I'd parked in front of the Wagon Wheel Café, pushed through the front door and settled in my usual spot at the pink and green Formica counter.

"What'll you have, Deputy?" Sal, the waitress, stood before me, her pen poised over her pad. Claiming not to be a day over sixty, she was a tall, thin woman who wore pink waitress uniforms and piled her brassy blond hair on top of her head.

I perused the menu more out of habit than necessity. "Guess I'll have a burger deluxe with the works and an order of fries." Sal turned to place my order. "Hang on a second," I said, looking at the menu again. "Can I also get a grilled cheese to go and a bottle of water?"

She gave me a quizzical look. "Plan on being hungry again real soon?"

"I have a passenger that needs a snack."

We both glanced out the front window at the Explorer, which appeared to be empty. Sal shrugged and moved off, and I leaned back in my seat only to be jolted by the sound of tires sliding on the gravel outside. I looked up just in time to see a metallic pink Cadillac skid to a stop behind my patrol vehicle. An elderly woman dressed in gray-checked pants and a black jacket climbed out and started for the front door; my heart skipped a beat as I recognized the bun of steel gray hair.

I'd met Marjorie Callaghan during a burglary investigation at the Surprise Valley Convalescent Hospital, and even though she helped apprehend the suspect, she'd practically crippled the poor woman in the process. She was demanding, often using her status as the mother of the mayor of Alturas to get her way. Not exactly the person I wanted to encounter by chance.

She charged through the double doors hard enough to send the small bell that hung at the top clanging against the glass, and immediately scanned the interior. "There you are, young woman," she said as soon as she spotted me.

"Mrs. Callaghan," I replied, half-rising from my seat as she approached. That's when I noticed she was no longer using a cane and had almost no limp. "You're getting around much better."

"Of course I am! I told those fool doctors I wouldn't need that long of a recovery from something as minor as hip surgery. Had enough of that convalescent hospital, so I checked myself out and went back home." She perched on the stool next to me. "Just started driving myself around this weekend, too. That's why I stopped. Some idiot has left a vehicle parked on the edge of the road just outside of Eagleville, and it's a real hazard. Didn't even get it off the pavement completely."

"What sort of vehicle is it?" I asked, pulling out my notebook.

"A Ford, I believe, older model with a camper shell. Hard to tell what color because it was very dirty."

I vaguely remembered seeing a vehicle fitting that description when I drove to Eagleville to investigate the missing alpaca, but I'd just assumed it belonged to some rancher. "I'll be happy to check it out, Mrs. Callaghan."

"See that you do before somebody runs into the back of it." With that she stood, tugged her short jacket into place, and marched out the door. I grimaced as she sped off, her car fishtailing and throwing gravel in all directions.

"Here you go, Hon," Sal said, setting before me a huge open-faced hamburger complete with lettuce, cheese, and a thick slice of tomato partially buried under a mound of golden french fries. "Cookie got these taters just right." She popped the remainder of one I was certain she'd liberated from my plate into her mouth. "I'll box up your grilled cheese and bring it out when you're ready to go."

"Thanks," I said, assembling my burger. Uncertain as to how long Bubbles would wait before chewing up my interior, I wasted no time consuming my lunch — down to the last fry. Sal met me at the cash register with a takeout box and a bottle of water.

"Hope your passenger..." She winked. "...likes this sandwich."

I smiled. "I'm sure he will. Thanks." Glancing over my shoulder on the way to my patrol unit, I spotted Sal in the front window, craning her neck for a better view.

As I opened the passenger door, Bubbles uncurled himself, stuck his rear end in the air and stretched. "Have a nice nap, you dumb dog? Here." I opened the box and set it on the floor. After tearing the sandwich into several pieces, I poured water into the other side. He jumped down and lapped up some before sniffing at the food and looking up at me. "That's it. You don't eat that, you go hungry." I closed the door and started around the back of the Explorer but stopped when I spied Pete coming out of the Silver Spur. Flashing on the kiss we'd shared on the shore of the reservoir, my face grew hot and my knees buckled, forcing me to lean against the vehicle. *Good grief, get a grip!* But before I could move, he saw me and waved.

"Hey, Sarah!" A broad grin lit up his face, and I imagined the twinkle of his crystal-blue eyes. He quickly looked both ways and then jogged across the street. "Have you heard anything about my ride?" he asked when he reached me.

I shook my head. "It's only been a few days, but something still might turn up."

"Man, I hope so. I put a lot of time and energy into that bike, and I'd really like to get it back."

He stepped closer and the faint hint of cologne, a warm earthy smell, drifted to my nose. I cleared my throat. "As soon as I hear anything, I'll call you."

"Yeah, I know you will." He moved even closer

and leaned on the rig next to me, his scent completely enveloping me. "If you don't have plans for Saturday, you should come to the Spur. It's open mic night, and that's always a good time."

"Huh?" *Not again.*

"Saturday, you should come to the Spur."

"Yeah, Saturday."

"Are you okay?" He pushed away from the Explorer and frowned at me.

"What, me? Yeah, I'm fine." I shook my head, trying to clear it. *Snap out of it!* I moved toward my door. "Well, I have to go. Need to check on some vehicle that's apparently a traffic hazard." I opened the door and climbed in behind the wheel, but Pete slid in next to me before I could close it.

"You sure you're okay?" His eyes searched mine. "You seem a little distracted."

If you only knew. "Just fine." I offered my most reassuring smile.

His grin reappeared. "Then I better let you go, Deputy." He stepped back and saluted. "See you Saturday." Before I could reply, he jogged back across the street and disappeared into the saloon.

After securing my seatbelt, I closed my door and started the Explorer. Then I backed out of my spot and headed for Eagleville, careful not to accelerate too quickly.

Twenty minutes later, I'd flipped a U-turn and pulled up behind the pickup Mrs. Callaghan had insisted was so dangerous. Hazard or not, it had been parked in the same place for several days, which seemed unusual considering that the back window of the camper shell was wide open.

"Come on, Bubbles," I said, climbing out. "While

I look things over, you can take a potty break." The small dog again jumped over the center console, bailed out of the unit, and trotted down the embankment.

When I reached the back of the truck, I pushed my sunglasses up onto my head and peered in through the open window. A huge wooden crate took up most of the bed, and its lid had been pried off and pushed to one side. A large cotton bag was partially draped over the side closest to the tailgate. Lowering my sunglasses back into place, I moved toward the passenger door, but as I reached for it, Bubbles began barking. Turning toward the sound, I saw nothing past the thick stand of willows growing along the stream that ran under the road and eventually emptied into Middle Lake.

"Here boy. Come." More barking. "Bubbles, stop that! Come here!" When the barking turned to growling, I decided to investigate.

I slipped down the gravel-covered slope and followed the curve of the stream, looking for a place to squeeze through the thicket. That's when I detected the familiar odor of decomposing flesh. Forcing my way through the slender branches, I expected to find the dog rolling on the carcass of some dead animal. What I found was definitely dead, but it wasn't an animal. The man was Caucasian, probably in his twenties, and lying supine a few feet from the water. I retrieved Bubbles and headed upstream toward the road but was blocked by a giant mass of wild rosebushes covering the embankment. Backtracking a little, I was able to escape the confinement of the willows and scrambled back up to the road. After securing the dog in the backseat of my unit,

I reached for the radio but changed my mind. Last time the call for a dead body went out, the location was inundated with lookyloos. Wanting to avoid that, I called dispatch on my cell phone instead.

"Hey Cindy. I've got an 11-44 just north of Eagleville."

"No shit! Do you need the coroner's van?"

"Affirmative. Also need a tow truck for an 11-24 that may be evidence."

"Got it. I'll dispatch both right away."

"Great, thanks."

Knowing it would take at least forty-five minutes for either vehicle to reach my location, I grabbed my evidence case and began processing the scene. I took pictures of the things in the bed of the truck as well as the open hatch of the camper shell. After donning a pair of latex gloves, I opened the passenger door and snapped some shots of the interior, including the layer of wrappers from a variety of fast food restaurants covering the floor and a single key in the ignition. The glove compartment held a tattered owner's manual but no registration or proof of insurance. Poking through the trash provided no clues, and the area under the seat revealed nothing more than a few greasy dust bunnies. With the truck thoroughly documented, the body was next.

Once again within the stand of willows, I began taking photographs. The sickening sweet stench of decay was intense. A faint breeze made it almost tolerable, but I felt my guts twist. I lowered the camera and stepped back. *Don't lose it! Shallow breaths.* While I gave my stomach a chance to settle, I surveyed the body and the surrounding area.

The man was dressed in gray plaid Bermuda

shorts so wrinkled he must have slept in them and a faded black T-shirt. Only one Teva sandal was still in place; the other one was nowhere in sight. His arms and legs were a strange hue of green, and blood vessels had created web-like patterns on the skin. The ground inside the stand of willows, which was covered with clumps of grass and large rocks, did not reveal drag marks or shoe prints. I had no idea what had happened or how he'd gotten there.

Ready to try again, I took a deep breath and held it while I finished photographing the scene. Last thing, I leaned in close to get a shot of his head, although I doubted anyone would recognize the swollen face with its bulging eyes. But as I zoomed in, the sight of tiny maggots writhing in the nose and corners of the mouth finished me off. I had just enough time to snap the picture before stumbling a few feet away and losing my lunch — down to the last fry.

Chapter 7

Reaching the Explorer moments later, I yanked open the passenger door, grabbed the bottle of water I'd bought for the dog, and drained it. I was still feeling queasy when Scott Jenkins pulled up in the unmarked, white coroner's van. A close friend from my high school rodeo days, Scott had told me about the opening at the Sheriff's Office when I'd come home to visit last Christmas.

"Hey Sarah," he called as he climbed out from behind the wheel. "Whatcha got going on?" He crossed the road and met me at the back of the pickup. "When Cindy put out the word you needed the van, I hightailed it back to the office as fast as I could. I definitely wanted in on any action..." He paused. "You okay? You're looking a little green around the gills."

I nodded. "Yeah, just give me another minute or two. Why don't you grab the Stokes litter and a body bag."

"Coming right up."

While he pulled the equipment out of the van, I went back and scouted for a place to carry the body through the willows but found nothing wide enough for at least a hundred yards. We needed a plan B.

"Hey where'd you go?" Scott called moments later.

"Hang on, I'll be right there." Moving back upstream toward the culvert, I spotted him standing on the roadside with the litter at his feet and immediately knew how to get the body out of the creek bed. "Grab a couple lengths of rope. We'll need to pull the body out over these bushes."

"You got it." He trotted back across the road and returned with a couple coils of Bluewater Safeline. As I waited for him to tie them off, I looked for the best place to drag the body across and spotted the missing Teva caught in the tangle of rosebushes, halfway up the embankment and just out of my reach.

"All set," Scott called, lowering the rescue basket. As soon as it reached the creek bed, he tossed me the ends of the rope. "What's the best way to get there?"

"Come down this way." I pointed to my right. "You'll have to squeeze between the willows." While he found his own way in, I hauled the equipment downstream.

"Man, he's a ripe one!" He'd reached the body first and was checking it out. "How long you think he's been here?"

"Judging by the skin and bloating, I'd say about three days," I said, setting down my load a few feet away. "That and the fact I saw his rig when I drove past here Saturday afternoon."

Scott's crooked smile slowly materialized. "Had me going for a second. So how're we gonna do this?"

Very carefully! The last body I'd recovered was smaller, partially skeletonized, and wearing pants and a long sleeve shirt, which made it easier to pick him up. This guy probably weighed close to two hundred thirty pounds and was in the early stages of putrefaction. "Well, we can try grabbing his arms and legs, but he looks a little..."

"Gooey!"

I nodded. "Maybe we can roll him into the body bag," I said reaching down and grabbing it, "and then get him into the litter that way."

"Works for me."

Within minutes we had the body bag open and into position, Scott on one side of the body and me on the other.

"Now we'll just sort of turn him over onto his stomach. Then one more time right into the bag." Using the belt loops of the shorts as handles, we slowly rolled him, but as soon as he was prone a huge release of intestinal gas erupted.

"Oh man, that's nasty!" Scott exclaimed, stepping back and waving his hand in front of his face. I was glad my stomach was already empty.

"Come on," I urged. "One more time and we'll have it in the bag, so to speak."

Scott's smile did not reappear. In fact, now *he* looked sick. Holding his breath, he moved back into position, and we flopped the body once more and zipped the bag as quickly as we could.

"Whew!" Scott raised his right arm and swiped at his sweaty brow with his shoulder. "Glad that's over with."

"But we still have to get him to the van," I reminded him.

Before he had a chance to argue, I grabbed the two handles near the victim's head and waited for him to grab the ones on his end. "Go on three. One, two, three." We lifted together, but the body bag never left the ground.

"Must be heavier than he looks," Scott said, letting go of the handles. "Swap ends with me. Maybe that'll work better."

Doubtful, I did what he suggested, and this time we managed to lift the bag a few inches before our arms gave out, and it hit the ground.

"Man, talk about dead weight!" He made another swipe at the beads of sweat forming on his forehead.

I snickered. It wasn't that funny — most of Scott's attempts at humor weren't — but I couldn't help it.

His crooked smile reappeared. "That was a pretty good one, huh?"

Still chuckling, I shook my head. "If we move the litter closer, I think we can heave him into it."

A quick adjustment and another attempt, we had the body ready to haul up to the road. Or so we thought. With the added weight of the Stokes litter, we couldn't budge it.

"Great! Now what?" Scott mopped his brow again. "If only we had another person." *Or at least a couple of lookyloos. Oh well.*

As if on cue, I heard the low whine of a diesel engine as it wound down. "I think you just got your wish." I tramped upstream and got to the road just as the tow truck was backing into position in front of the abandoned vehicle.

"Howdy Sarah," the driver called as he came around the back of his rig. Immediately I recognized the burly man as Cindy's uncle, owner of the only tire shop in Alturas as well as the small motel where I'd stayed.

"Hey Bert, am I glad to see you. Deputy Jenkins and I need your help."

"Okay. Where do you want me?"

"Come down over there." I gestured to the right for a second time. "Push through the willows and head downstream."

"Gotcha!" The large man lumbered down the bank and trudged along the outside of the willow stand. "How the hell did you get in there?" he called.

"You'll have to squeeze through somewhere," I answered, keeping pace with him.

"Squeeze through? For the love of..." The willows between us began to quiver and crack. Two large hands appeared and parted the branches like a bead curtain, and Cindy's Uncle Bert shoved his massive body through. "Now what's so doggone important I had to do that?" he said, straightening the ball cap that had been knocked askew.

"You'll see." I led the way downstream, and as we drew closer to where Scott was waiting, I heard Bert sniff at the air a couple of times.

"Is that what I think it is?" he asked. Then he murmured something I didn't understand, but the tone told me he wasn't too pleased.

An hour later, we'd managed to get the body hauled over the rosebushes, thanks to Bert's idea to use his winch, and loaded into the van. The abandoned vehicle was much easier to secure on the flatbed of the tow truck, and an old tire iron discovered on the ground under the pickup explained how the lid of the wooden box had been pried off. However, I still didn't know the cause of death or how he ended up along the creek bed so far from the road. Scott and Bert drove off to deliver their cargos while I waited for the dumb dog to finish relieving himself.

"Come on Bubbles," I called, anxious to head over the pass myself. A few seconds later, the miniature mutt appeared at my feet, leapt into the Explorer, and stood in the passenger seat with his front paws braced against the armrest, his tail wagging in anticipation. *Good grief!*

I caught the other two vehicles on the downhill-side of Cedar Pass and followed them into Alturas. By the time we got to the Sheriff's Office, I was ready for a shower and something to eat, neither of which would be happening any time soon.

"Well?" Cindy asked the second I rounded the corner by her dispatcher's desk.

"Well what?"

She rolled her chair closer to where I was leaning against the tall, circular counter that surrounded her desk. "What's the scoop on the dead guy? How did he die? Was it an accident or something more sinister? Was he murdered there or was it a body dump? Any clues in the vehicle? What kind of vehicle is it? How long do you think he's been there? Who..."

"Whoa!" I held up my hands. "Too many questions!"

"Come on, Sarah. Start talking. I want all the details."

"Okay, okay. Here's what I know, or more like what I don't know. Don't know how he died or how he got where he was. Therefore, don't know if it was an accident or not. The vehicle was an old beater truck with a camper shell. I saw no clues in the truck other than a huge wooden box and cloth bag, and I have no idea why they were in the back."

"What about the guy? Was he from around here?"

"Don't think so, the truck had expired Nevada plates. *Another thing I'd missed the first time I'd seen it.* Should know more after Josh gets done processing it." Josh Green was the only lab tech for the Modoc County Sheriff's Department and very skilled at what he did. "He and your uncle Bert are unloading it now. And someone needs to drive the body to Redding for an autopsy."

"Gotcha." Cindy swiveled to her computer. "You get the paperwork going and I'll dispatch a deputy." She checked the duty roster and began typing on her keyboard. "And what do you say to a beer and an extra large Sicilian pizza at Antonio's?"

My stomach growled. Antonio's Italien Restaurant served up authentic Italian cuisine, which included the best homemade pizza in the county.

"Sounds great. I should be ready in about forty-five minutes."

"Great, I'll call and reserve our favorite table."

Seated at a small table in the back of Antonio's, Cindy and I had consumed half the pizza and were working on our second round of beer. Having explained the dog dilemma, I'd taken a piece to Bubbles along with some water and, after letting him out for another pee break, left him curled up on the passenger seat.

"Ran into Pete this morning." I selected another slice.

"Oh?"

"Yeah, he asked about his bike and then invited me to open mic night at the Silver Spur this Saturday."

57

"What's that?"

"Not sure, but he tells me it's always a good time. Perhaps we should check it out?"

"I don't know." She chugged most of her beer. "He's not really my type."

I flashed on Pete's kiss again. "Uh, well..." I took a huge bite of pizza and slowly chewed. He may not be my type either, but I figured it was worth investigating. I swallowed. "...I think I'll go, in case you change your mind."

"Maybe. Hey, want to come over for a while? I got a new movie from Netflix."

I checked my watch; it was after seven, and I was at least an hour away from home. "I need to get going. That dumb dog has been in my rig all day, and I could use a shower." We split what was left of the pizza, said our good-byes, and I headed over Cedar Pass. Fifty minutes later, I pulled into Remy's driveway.

"Come on Dog, let's see if you have a place to stay tomorrow." I plodded up the steps and knocked on the door. Sounds of Gordon Lightfoot drifted out from inside, bringing with it the faint smell of fried bacon. I was about to knock again when Remy jerked open the door.

"Well, howdy there. I was hoping you might..." He glanced down at my feet, "Oh shit!" and slammed the door.

Confused, I stood there until I realized what had upset him. "Remy!" I knocked again. "It's just me. She's not here." Last time my sister came for a visit, they didn't get along so well, and I guessed he was still a little gun-shy.

Slowly, the door opened just a crack. "That there's her dog, ain't it?"

"Yes but Alexis didn't bring it. She had the dog shipped, so I'm stuck watching the mutt while she's away."

The door opened about a foot and my neighbor and self-proclaimed partner poked his head out, looking first to the right and then to the left. "Well if you're sure." He stepped back and opened the door all the way. "Come on in." Before I could move, Bubbles trotted by me, sniffed around the room, and proceeded to make himself comfortable in Remy's favorite chair.

"Oops, sorry." I hustled over and picked up the dog. "Actually I stopped by to ask if you wouldn't mind keeping an eye on Bubbles while I'm patrolling." I set him down and pointed. "Sit, stay." Just like before, he dropped his butt to the floor and waited.

"What in tarnation! You teach her that?"

I shook my head. "And — she's a he."

"Well, I'll be damned."

Chapter 8

The next day I left Bubbles with Remy and headed south, patrolling to the Nevada border. As I drove through the maze of county roads east of Eagleville, the radio remained silent. No emergencies or disasters to report, and I'd almost reached the main road when something caught my eye.

With childlike anticipation of a Christmas morning, I pulled over and jumped out of the Explorer. Still uncertain of what I'd seen and not wanting to scare it off, I crept toward the large sagebrush where I was sure something was hiding. Using my best stealth skills, I circled the bush and tackled the small animal before it knew I was there. With my captive held tightly in my arms, I hustled back to my unit and shoved the animal into the back compartment. That's when I realized it wasn't the missing cria.

The small, snow-white goat was about the right size, but that's where the similarities ended. No tightly kinked coat and no long neck. And unlike the quiet creatures I'd encountered on the alpaca ranch, this small member of the goat family was making its displeasure known. The bleating started the instant I let go and didn't sound like it would be stopping any time soon. I slammed the cargo door shut and looked around; the nearest ranch was at least a half-mile away. Hesitant to leave the small animal to potential predators, I had no choice but to take it with me, so I slid in behind the wheel and drove north. By the time I reached Cedarville, my stomach was making almost as much noise as the goat but stopping to get something to eat wasn't an option. Pushing on, I arrived at Remy's about one o'clock.

"Didn't expect you to be back so soon?" he called, coming out the front door of his mobile home with Bubbles right behind him.

"Me either." I threw open the rear door and liberated my noisy captive. "But I had to deal with this."

"Where the hell did that come from?" Remy asked as he joined me at the back of the rig.

"Thought it was the missing alpaca I've been watching for."

"Al who?"

"Alpaca. You know, kinda like a llama?"

Bubbles circled the small goat, and then the two touched noses. An obvious friendship established, they trotted off together.

"Well, would ya look at that?" Remy watched the pair until they disappeared behind the woodshed. "So, whatcha gonna do with the little fella?"

"Take its picture and make some flyers," I said, fishing my digital camera out of the evidence case. "It must belong to someone." I pulled the hatch closed and started off after the animals.

"But what are you gonna to do with it in the meantime?" Remy asked, keeping pace with me.

"Well, I suppose I could put it..." But I didn't have an answer. I halted and looked at him. "I have no idea." As I spoke my mind raced, searching for any possible place on my property to secure such a small animal, but the barbed wire surrounding the pasture was too widely spaced. "I guess I could lock it in Raven's stall," I offered.

"That might work." His frown told me otherwise. "Course the old hencoop may do the trick," he said, nodding toward the garden.

Turning around, I spotted a small structure surrounded by chicken wire. Apparently Peggy's affection for roosters went beyond her kitchen decorations. The enclosure was full of waist-high weeds, but the fencing appeared sturdy. "Oh that would be much better. And it should only be for a couple of days. Are you sure you don't mind?"

Remy beamed. "Not a bit. Besides, it'll give the pooch someone to play with, and he won't be underfoot all the time." After snapping a few pictures, I drove to my place, leaving Remy to wrestle the goat into the chicken coop.

With a few quick clicks on my computer, the flyers printed while I made myself a peanut butter and apple sandwich. Grabbing a bottle of water to go with it and the stack of flyers, I was back on the road and headed for Cedarville.

By mid-afternoon, I'd put up flyers outside the Wagon Wheel Café, Silver Spur Saloon, Morrison's Mercantile, and the corner gas station. I continued south and posted two more at the Eagleville General Store and the auto repair shop. After that I started for home, finishing my patrol on County Road 17 as far as Lake City and then on to Fort Bidwell via the main road.

Having collected Bubbles from Remy and declined

an invitation to dinner, I hurried home and popped a frozen chicken entrée into the microwave. While it heated, I stripped off my uniform, pulled on a pair of grey sweats and an oversized T-shirt, and practically fell over my sister's dog as I reentered the kitchen. "Stupid dog! Get out of the way."

Unshaken, Bubbles watched from his spot in the middle of the kitchen floor as I checked my food and nuked it for another two minutes. Thinking he might be hungry, I changed his water and put out more dog food. Then I relocated to my office to end my day doing paperwork, my dinner balanced on a potholder in one hand and a beer in the other.

I slipped the memory card from my camera into the photo printer, and as it spit out the pictures I'd taken, I flipped through my notebook. I'd seen more action in four days that most deputies see in four months; a stolen motorcycle, a missing animal, a dead body and a recovered animal that may not be missing — yet. And in every incident there had been no clues. Well almost no clues. There had been boot prints around Pete's bike, but I'd neglected to take pictures of them, and with the missing cria, there'd been nothing to take pictures of. I'd taken several of the pickup and dead guy but didn't notice anything of consequence. *Am I losing my edge?* Josh might find something, or the autopsy may give me some answers on cause of death, but that would take some time.

In between bites of chicken Alfredo and draws on my beer, I typed up what few notes I had and opened my email. The only message in my inbox was from Sue James, and it was marked urgent. Draining the last of my beer, I clicked on it, and three words, written all in capitals, leapt out at me.

"IT WASN'T HENSLEY!!"

There was more written below that, but I needed another beer before reading it. I tossed the remnants of my dinner into the trash and grabbed the last beer out of the fridge. *If Hensley isn't dead, where the hell is he?*

Richard Hensley was a rogue. A former FBI agent, he'd flipped out after getting fired from the Bureau because his refusal to request backup resulted in a shootout that almost cost a rookie his life. He threatened the deputy director and accused me of falsifying my report. Shortly after I resigned and moved back to California, he'd vanished. Missing for almost a month, his car had been found, but it and the body inside had been incinerated. Sue told me they weren't sure if it was Hensley or not — until now.

Settled once again in front of my computer, I read the rest of Sue's message.

> The deputy director wanted a positive ID but the body was too badly burned. They couldn't get DNA or fingerprints, but they know it wasn't him. The blackened skull had all its teeth — no sign of Hensley's gold crowns. They did find the melted residue of a .357 bullet but no gun. The guys investigating this think Hensley killed that person in order to fake his own death. Be careful! He's now wanted by the FBI!!

I read through it twice. I'd spent enough time

with Richard Hensley, having slept with him over a year ago, to know he could be a real asshole, but this was bizarre, even for him.

While my computer shut down, I organized the new photos and added them to my evidence wall. Then I chugged the last of my beer, making a mental note to pick up some more tomorrow on the way home, grabbed my robe, and headed for the bathhouse. "Come on, Dog. Can't leave you here alone."

With the miniature mutt in tow, I hung up my robe and turned on the hose. As the deliciously warm water began to fill the hot tub, I tramped down to the barn to feed Raven. Not wanting to risk freaking out the gelding again, I paused at the gate and told Bubbles, "Sit, stay!" As before, the dog's haunches hit the ground. Keeping an eye on him, I tossed Raven a flake of hay. Rubbing his massive neck as he nibbled, I contemplated my recent picnic with a certain bartender until I was sure the tub was filled at least halfway. Then I bid my equine friend good-bye and returned to the bathhouse, my canine nuisance close behind.

The water had climbed up the side of the tub even further than I'd predicted and, as I shrugged out of my clothes, the Shorkie began pacing back and forth, barking. "Hush up Bubbles," I scolded. Closing my eyes and sinking into the steamy water, I was startled by a sudden splash; I had been joined by my four-legged houseguest.

My first reaction was to fish him out and toss him through the small window. But the way he paddled around, taking an occasional lick of the mineral-saturated water was too comical to interrupt, so we shared the tub until I was pruny, and he was exhausted.

Chapter 9

The first thing I noticed pulling into Remy's drive-way Wednesday morning was the open gate of the chicken coop. *Where the hell's that goat now?* Leaving Bubbles to wander around, I climbed the front steps and knocked.

"Morning Remy," I said when he pulled the door open. "Did you know the goat's missing?"

"Ain't missing." He stood back, giving me a clear view into his place. The creature in question was curled up on a folded blanket next to Remy's fa-vorite chair. "Goldarn thing wouldn't shut up 'til I brought it inside." I suspected differently but didn't challenge him.

"Not sure how late I'll be today. I have to patrol the back country on the north end of the valley. Most of it is narrow dirt road, so it'll be slow going." I stepped back, and Remy joined me on the front porch. Together we moved down the steps and to-ward the Ford Explorer. Bubbles trotted over and was snatched up by the caregiver of the doggie day-care, who deftly rotated the dog and tucked him un-der his right arm, just as I'd seen Alexis do a dozen times. Fighting the urge to laugh, I waved good-bye and slid in behind the wheel. Practically hysterical,

I started the vehicle, drove out of Remy's driveway and immediately began the climb out of the valley as I headed up Highgrade Road.

Grateful the more remote areas were patrolled less frequently, I made good time on the gravel-packed road until I reached the tree line. There the road narrowed, and the twists and turns required more concentration. The potholed-filled obstacle course forced me to reduce speed until I finally drove down the steep grade into Cave Lake Campground, where camping in tents, boiling the drinking water, and watching for marauding bears were the only disadvantages. Fantastic fishing, cave exploration, and staying for free were the benefits. Even so, only one campsite was occupied, but it was still early in the year. Not to mention freezing cold at night.

Continuing my patrol, I cruised by the tiny twin lakes nearby. Both were unoccupied, eerily silent, and appropriately named. Water lilies dotted the surface of Lily Lake, and a jagged opening into the hillside glared across Cave Lake, as if cautioning intruders to stay away. Heeding the warning, I headed back the way I'd come until I reached the rubble pile of a mine abandoned long ago. Turning left, I followed the road as it meandered through the trees past Moonlight Mine and on toward Dismal Swamp. Like a scene from William Goldman's *The Princess Bride*, the wetland area is covered by oversized vegetation, crystal clear streams, and trees sporting limbs more dead than alive. Had Remy been riding along, I probably would have warned him about R.O.U.S.

By twelve o'clock, I'd driven out of the swamp, across a vast mountain meadow and into a high desert-like region on the Oregon border. Tired of sitting, I pulled over and took a short walk to stretch my legs. On the way back to my unit, I heard a strange noise. It reminded me of the wounded rabbit call my dad used when we'd hunt coyotes. Trying to pinpoint where the sound originated, I began walking in an ever-widening circle, but it was intermittent and hard to detect. I'd just about given up when I heard it again coming from a huge patch of stinging nettles nearby.

Carefully pinching a leave with each hand so as to avoid the stinging hairs, I pulled the branches apart and peered inside. A fawn, its spots still clearly visible, was curled into a tight ball and immediately fell silent as soon as its big brown eyes saw me. Stepping back, I scanned the area for its mother but found nothing. Then I circled the patch of vegetation. The only sign I detected was a trail of tracks that had to be several days olds. Concerned for the animal's well-being, I decided to haul it out of the stinging nettles and check it out.

I pulled the utility jumpsuit out of the back of my unit and stepped into it. After tugging on two pairs of latex gloves, I was ready to move in. Being careful not to let the plants touch my face, I pushed my way into the thick vegetation.

Startled, the small deer attempted to escape but couldn't get to its feet. Taking advantage of the situation, I bent down and scooped the animal into my arms. But when I turned to go back the way I'd come, I failed to see a rogue branch of nettles in my path. The searing pain was instantaneous as it brushed across my left cheek, and swiping it on my shoulder only made it worse.

Blinded by tears of pain, I stumbled to the Explorer and managed to shove the deer into the rear compartment. Ripping off the latex gloves, I moved to the passenger door, pulled it open, and grabbed one of the bottles of water I'd packed for the trip. I poured some into my left hand and scrubbed my face. After doing this three or four times, the burning sensation began to fade, and I could see again. Taking what was left in the bottle and an apple out of my lunch, I went back to the rear of the vehicle.

The fawn remained where I'd left it. I reached out and stroked its head and back. As I did so, I gently pinched at the skin over its spine. Instead of quickly falling back into place, it stayed where it was for a few seconds before slowly flattening out again — a sure sign of severe dehydration. *Poor little thing must have been on its own for days.*

Setting down the apple, I poured some water into my hand and offered it to the deer. Leery at first, it finally drank all I had to give it. Then I pulled out my Swiss army knife and cut the apple into tiny bites. Slowly the small animal ate every morsel, then laid its head down and closed its eyes.

Hopeful it would survive, I stripped off the jumpsuit, closed the rear door, and climbed in behind the wheel. Negotiating the road as quickly as possible, I drove back to Remy's and pulled into his driveway an hour later. *How am I going to explain this?*

Opening the back of my patrol unit, my heart sank. The fawn hadn't moved at all, nor did it flinch when I touched it. "Damn it!" I turned around, leaned against the rig, and folded my arms across my chest.

"What the heck you doing?" Remy called as he

came around the side of his mobile home, followed closely by his two charges. "Thought you were gonna be gone all day." He stopped in front of me and peered into the vehicle. "That what I think it is?"

"Yeah," I kept my eyes focused at the ground. "I came across it, but I think it's been alone too long to survive."

He pushed his black felt hat to the back of his head and leaned in closer. "Looks fine to me."

"Huh?" I studied him, not sure what he was saying.

Remy smiled and nodded toward the fawn. "I said it looks all right to me."

Spinning around, I was relieved to see the small animal on its feet and staring at us. Slowly I reached in, cradled it in my arms, and lifted it out of the rig. "Okay to put it in the pen? Just for now?"

"Don't see why not. Millie ain't gonna be using it."

"Really appreciate this." We headed for the small enclosure. "I'll call — Millie?" I stopped. "Who's Millie?"

Remy chuckled. "Named the goat Millie, after my tiny white-haired granny. Didn't see no harm, had to call it something besides Goat. And what'd you do to that face of yours this time?" he asked, jerking his chin at me.

"Stinging nettles," I replied.

The fawn was getting heavy, so I started for the pen again. After securing it inside, I sent Remy in search of something for it to eat. In the meantime, I returned to my patrol unit and called the Bureau of Land Management, hoping to find someone to advise me on how to care for an orphaned fawn. A few minutes later, I had a page of information written in my notebook and went looking for the keeper of the menagerie. I found him chopping carrots in the kitchen.

"This should be useful in caring for the fawn." I tore the page from my notebook and laid it on the red-checkered tablecloth.

Remy dried his hands on a dishtowel decorated with a huge rooster, picked up the small piece of paper, and read it. "Lotta fuss for one little critter." He stuffed the paper into his shirt pocket and went back to chopping. "Figured I'd care for it like the bummer lambs we used to raise on my dad's ranch."

"Well, whatever you decide to do, it should only be for a little while. Someone from the BLM is supposed to get back to me and arrange a pickup. Until then, I'll get some goat feed at the farm supply tomorrow as I pass through Cedarville."

"That and these here fruit and veggies outta do the trick." He scraped the bite-size morsels of the orange vegetable into a large pot, on top of a couple of cut up apples.

"Looks like you've got things under control, so I'll get back to work. I still have quite a bit of country to patrol."

Determined to finish my day without any more complications, I munched my sandwich on the way to Lake Annie and washed it down with my last bottle of water. Continuing past the small body of water, which actually resembled a gigantic pond rather than a tiny lake, I followed the narrow dirt road until it hooked up with County Road 1. From there I drove north until I reached the Oregon border for the second time that day. Then I turned around and headed back to Fort Bidwell. No stopping to stretch my legs or look around. No lost animals to deal with. At 5:30 I'd reached the tiny town and was heading for the General Store on the corner of Bridge and Willow Streets.

Before going in, I removed my gun belt and stowed it under the front seat. Next I shrugged out of my uniform shirt, released the Velcro straps on my body armor and traded it for the lightweight jacket I keep under the center console. Feeling more dressed down, I went inside.

More like a stop 'n shop at a gas station, the small block building housed a limited selection of miniature cans and bottles of name brand products, a variety of chips in the grab and go size, a few loaves of bread, and a fairly decent choice of sodas in sixteen ounce bottles. The only product in endless supply was beer. Four of the five refrigerated units were full of it as well as the shelves across the aisle. Lager, ale, or dark — it had them all.

Sticking with the basics, I selected a twelve-pack of Miller High Life out of the middle cooler. Tired of peanut butter and apple sandwiches, I also grabbed a loaf of rye bread, a package of sliced salami and cheese, and a jar of brown mustard. With my purchases stashed on the floor behind my seat, I drove to Remy's.

Pulling into his driveway, I wasn't surprised to see Bubbles and Millie pressed against the small pen, nose to nose with the fawn. Figuring Remy would be close by, I parked the Explorer and wandered around the side of the mobile home where I found him hacking at weeds with a large hoe. His red plaid shirt and black felt hat had been abandoned and hung on a nearby post.

"Looks like you've been hard at it," I said as I approached.

"Aaaaa!!" He jumped hard, practically throwing the hoe over his shoulder. "What in tarnation you doin' sneaking up on me like that! 'Bout gave me a heart attack!"

"Oh Remy..." I began to laugh. "...I didn't mean to. Really!" My laughter grew in intensity, even though I tried suppressing it.

"Don't see what's so damn funny, scaring an old man half to death." He threw down the hoe and stomped over to where his hat and shirt were hanging.

"Remy, I'm really sorry. I didn't mean to scare you!" I followed him up onto the back porch. "And I didn't mean to laugh. It's just..." Another giggled escaped. "...you really jumped!" I clamped both hands over my mouth and shook my head.

My neighbor stood glaring at me, his hands on his hips. All of a sudden, he burst out laughing. "I sure did, didn't I?" He jammed his hat on his head and slipped his shirt on over his white T-shirt. "Come on in. I've got dinner all ready." He turned toward the small pen and let out a shrill whistle. The two small animals on the outside snapped to attention and then raced toward us. Within seconds, they were underfoot.

"Hold on there," Remy scolded, "let me get the door opened." With barely enough room to get through, Bubbles and Millie rushed in, taking up strategic positions so as to not miss out on anything.

"I appreciate the offer," I said following him into the house, "but I need to get home."

"Nonsense. I made plenty. Now grab yourself a beer and set a spell."

I started to argue, but the delicious smell of something filled my nostrils. "Mmm, what are you cooking?"

"Dump chicken," Remy said as he hung his hat on its hook by the front door.

I stopped midstride. "You're cooking sea gull?"

"Sea gull? What in tarnation gave you the idea I was cooking sea gull?" He buttoned his shirt on his way back into the kitchen.

"When I was a kid, that's what my dad used to call the sea gulls at the dump."

He chuckled and shook his head. "Nope. No sea gull. Just a chicken and some salsa dumped in on top of it. Found the recipe in the Sunday paper a while back. Nothin' fancy but it'll fill the void." He scooped the contents of the crock pot into a large bowl, picking out the bones as he went, and I dug a couple of beers out of the fridge. "Bring out that plate of fixins while you're in there," he ordered, pulling a foil packet out of the oven. Then he picked up a good-sized chicken bone and a chunk of apple he had cut up on a small plate. "Here you go." He gave the bone to Bubbles and Millie got the apple. "Now make yourselves scarce." To my amazement, the pair trotted into the living room, plopped down on the blanket, and began chomping on their treats.

"Got any leads on Pete's motorcycle?" Remy asked as he piled chicken and the fixings on a flour tortilla.

"How'd you know about that?"

"Heard it straight from the horse's mouth." I must have looked confused because he chuckled and added, "Ran into Pete this morning when I made a run to Morrison's Mercantile, and he filled me in." He rolled the tortilla into a humungous burrito and took a bite.

"Not a clue, just like with the missing alpaca and the dead body," I said, rolling my own tortilla into a smaller version of the same burrito.

"Dead body?" That's when he began choking, but before I could do anything, he waved me away, grabbed his beer and chugged it. When he could breathe again, he said, "What dead body?"

Chapter 10

Thursday's patrol took me back to Fee Reservoir, and I couldn't keep from smiling as I drove past the table where Pete and I'd shared our impromptu picnic. Traveling along the eastern side of Upper Lake, narrow dirt roads not much better than a bike trail made my journey tedious, and by the time I pulled onto Highway 299, across from the High Desert Hot Springs, I felt as dry and dusty as my patrol unit looked. Turning right, I drained my last bottle of water and headed for Cedarville.

As I drove down the extra wide Main Street, I noticed a group of teenagers washing the area's fire truck and rescue unit, which were parked in front of the fire hall.

"Hey Deputy," one of the boys called, waving a giant soapy sponge. It was Billy Hendrickson, his shock of red hair easily recognizable.

"Hi Billy." I slowed to a stop. "What are you boys up to today?"

"Us scouts are doing community service." He gestured at my rig. "Looks like you could use a wash yourself. Park alongside the engine here, and we'll get you all cleaned up."

Willing to support the group's efforts and

acknowledging my vehicle's need for a bath, I eased it into line, got out, and walked the two blocks to the feed store. It felt good to stretch my legs after being cooped up in my patrol unit for the better part of the last two days. I paid for the bag of goat food, asked to have it hauled to the Explorer, and walked to the mercantile across the street. There I ordered a turkey sandwich from the small deli and grabbed a six-pack of Mountain Dew for the kids and a diet Pepsi for myself. As I waited for my sandwich, I spotted a small tray of enchiladas ready to bake. Building on that, I added a can of refried beans and a bag o'salad to my basket. *Dinner.*

By the time I got back to the fire hall, my rig was sparkling clean and the kids, now hot and sweaty, eagerly accepted the sodas I had to offer.

"Thanks guys, it looks great." I set my own soda and sandwich on the center console, opened the back of the Explorer, and placed the bag of stuff for my dinner next to the sack of goat food. Then I backed out and drove to the park two blocks west of Main Street.

After making a much needed trip to the public restroom, I ate my lunch and planned out the remainder of my day, which included a long soak in the hot tub, Mexican cuisine, and holding down the sofa with the help of a miniature mutt. *Perfect!*

The first indicator that Friday was going to be a bitch of a day was the failure of my alarm to do its job. Having overslept for more than an hour, I threw on my uniform without bothering to strap on my body armor or tuck in my shirt. No time to braid my hair, so I secured it in an elastic at the nape of my neck and stomped into my work boots, leaving the laces untied. Then I slung my gun belt over my shoulder, shoved my body armor under one arm and Bubbles under the other, and headed out the door, grabbing the autopsy report I'd received the night before off the printer tray as I went by. A few minutes later, I pulled into Remy's driveway and, after letting Bubbles out of the vehicle, I had just enough time to get my armor into place and adjust my shirt before he and Millie burst out the front door.

"Thought maybe you'd taken the day off."

"No I had an alarm malfunction." I began braiding my hair, pulling it to one side to finish. "Probably play catch-up all day."

"I 'spect so," Remy said, scratching his chin through the coarse white hair of his beard. "Thanks for picking up that goat feed. That l'il fella out there gobbles it right up." He nodded toward the pen, where the trio stood nose to nose once again.

"Good. That bag should last until someone comes to collect the fawn." I bent down and laced up my boots.

"Don't see how that's necessary. It's doing just fine right here."

I checked my watch; I didn't have time to argue. "We'll talk about it later. I really have to get going." I opened my door, but before I could get in, my cell phone went off. "Deputy Murdock."

"Bob Robertson here, and this has got to stop!"

"What has to stop Mr. Robertson?"

"Another one of my damn crias is missing!" His screaming forced me to hold the phone away from my ear. "Someone is going to pay for this!"

"I'll be there as soon as I can." I clicked my phone

off and shoved it back in my pocket. "Looks like I'm headed to Eagleville."

"Maybe this time there'll be some kind of evidence, some clue as to what the hell is going on."

"Evidence!" I reached in through the open door and retrieved the autopsy report I'd tossed onto the dash.

"Whatcha got there?" Remy moved in closer.

"Autopsy report on my John Doe. Got it last night, but I haven't had a chance to read it." Scanning, I learned the victim was a 20-year-old named Chris Aldrich, last known address in Bishop, California. He'd been arrested eighteen months prior for possession of marijuana with intent to sell, but that was it. Skipping down to the bottom, I looked for the cause of death. "Says here petechial hemorrhages were present in the conjunctivae of the eyes but a lack of ligature marks on the neck and no hyoid bone fractures indicated that the victim did not die of strangulation but rather death was due to mechanical asphyxia."

"What in tarnation is mechanical asphyxia?" Remy asked.

"Took the words right out of my mouth. I know asphyxia means not breathing but not sure about the mechanical part."

"What the heck is that?" Remy pointed to one of the photographs on the next page.

"I'm not sure. Looks like pinpricks in the skin. Let me see what the description says." I flipped back to the front page and looked for the section on the external examination. "V-shaped punctures on the right forearm and head, the base of the wound measuring four inches across and approximately six inches in length, but the cause is unknown." I looked at the photograph again. "You ever see anything like this?" I asked Remy.

He shook his head. "Can't say as I have."

"Just great. More questions than answers." I folded up the report and tossed it back on the dashboard of the Explorer. Then I slid in behind the wheel and started the engine. "Wish me luck," I said before pulling the door closed and driving away.

Pulling into the Robertson's driveway forty-five minutes later, an overwhelming feeling of déjà vu washed over me. The rancher was again standing in front of his house, arms folded across his chest. The only difference this time was he approached my vehicle and jerked open my door before I could put the Explorer in park and shut off the engine.

"I don't know what is going on, but I want my animals found and someone put in jail," he demanded.

"I understand Mr. Robertson." I climbed out and strapped on my gun belt. "I'll look around again."

"It won't do no good. I've already looked, and there is nothing out of the ordinary. It's like they've vanished into thin air!"

Another tour of the field and I had to agree, not one wire cut or bent, not a single blade of grass flattened or out of place, and a LGD that was strangely silent. Nothing unusual, that is, until I pulled to the end of the gravel driveway, where I spotted a short, stocky man wearing bib overalls almost faded to white with a red union suit underneath.

As I came to a stop, he stepped up to my patrol unit. "Morning," I said after lowering the passenger-side window. "I'm looking into the disappearance of some alpacas. Have you noticed anything strange going on?"

"Ayup." The man nodded once.

"You know what happened to them?" I couldn't believe my luck. An eyewitness.

"Ayup." He shoved his hands deep in his pockets. "Aliens!" With that he turned around and began walking south.

My day went downhill from there!

Chapter 11

Peering into the mirror above the bathroom sink Saturday evening, I was pleased to see my face looked almost normal. The Armorall rash was gone and the mark left behind by the stinging nettle hardly noticeable. Deciding what to do with my hair was more of a concern. Accustomed to wearing it in a single braid down my back, nothing I did to it seemed to look right. Finally, I just let it hang loosely about my shoulders. Pulling on jeans and a cap sleeved T-shirt, I was ready to go.

"Okay Dog," I said, addressing the ball of fur that had made itself comfortable on my bed. "I'm trusting you to be on your best behavior while I'm gone." The tail wagged in acknowledgment, but I had my doubts. Not wanting to take a chance on Bubbles getting bored, I turned on the television and tuned it to our favorite channel before heading out the door.

By the time I got to the Silver Spur Saloon, open mic night was in full swing, and the closest place to park was two blocks away. As I approached the door, the fast beat of a tambourine and lyrics that sounded vaguely familiar greeted me. It wasn't until the female singer began the chorus, loud and off-key, that I recognized "Walking on Sunshine."

Inside, the noise level was deafening. People were crammed into every available crevice and shouting at each other in an attempt to carry on casual conversations. Spotting Pete in his typical two-tone bowling shirt and black jeans, my pulse rate increased as I navigated my way through the crowd to an open spot at the bar.

He flashed his big smile and moved toward me, his earthy cologne reaching me a second before he did. Leaning close he hollered, "So glad you made it. What can I get you?"

"How about a beer?" I yelled back, resting one foot on the brass rail that ran along the base of the huge mahogany bar.

"Coming right up." He turned around and reached into the refrigerated unit under the shelf of hard liquor. "Bud or Corona?" he asked placing a bottle of each in front of me.

Unable to compete with the dull roar of the crowd, I tapped the top of the clear bottle, which he opened with the practiced hand of a seasoned bartender. "Is it always this crazy on open mic night?" I asked after the song ended.

"Yep. It's like they come out of the woodwork." He returned the other bottle of beer to the cooler. "Hey Shellie," he called to the woman helping him tend bar. "When you get a second, come here. I'd like you to meet someone."

She waved and nodded. About my height, she wore an ankle-length skirt that flowed beneath a long sleeve shirt, and her textured, honey-colored hair just touched her shoulders. Although I couldn't see her feet, I was willing to bet she had on sandals of some sort. With a sudden pang of jealousy, I estimated her age to be close to mine.

"Shellie, this is Deputy Sarah," Pete said as she joined us.

"Pleased to meet you." She held out her hand, and I was surprised at the coolness of her skin. Looking into her face, I was relieved that I'd underestimated her age by about thirty years. "She's a beautiful green edged in blue," she told him.

I looked down at my brown shirt and frowned. "Sorry?"

"Remember? I mentioned Shellie reads auras," he said, grinning at me again.

I nodded.

She placed her hand on Pete's shoulder. "And his is bright orange. Perfect for a bartender, don't you think? Now if you'll excuse me, I see I'm needed at my end of the bar." A swish of her long skirt and a hint of patchouli, she returned to the waiting patrons. Before I could question Pete further, he tended to his own thirsty customers.

Slipping onto a newly abandoned barstool, I watched with mild curiosity as one of Pete's band members set up an electronic keyboard on the small stage. As he made some final adjustments, a lanky cowboy and a young girl in a tank top and tight Wranglers joined him and traded sheet music for a couple of microphones. After a brief piano introduction, they broke into "Don't Go Breaking My Heart." By the time they reached the first "Ooh hoo," everyone in the place was quiet.

"They're pretty good, aren't they?" Pete's question startled me; I hadn't seen him move in behind me.

I nodded. "Certainly wasn't expecting that song," I said, turning around on the barstool to face him. "A country duet maybe, but not Elton John."

He smiled. "They're here almost every time and like to mix it up a bit. Last time they sang 'Yesterday.' The crowd loves them." As if to prove his point, thunderous applause erupted when the duo finished.

"Are all the performers that good?" I asked when it had quieted down.

Pete looked toward the stage and chuckled. "Not exactly," he said, shaking his head.

Following his gaze, I saw a man of average build making his way to the stage, a large acoustic guitar in one hand and a short stool in the other. As he made himself comfortable, conversations throughout the bar resumed. Without strumming a note he began. "You painted up your lips and rolled and curled your tinted hair..." After a brief pause, he started vigorously strumming his guitar and continued singing the Kenny Rogers hit. His playing was only slightly better than his singing, but both were so atrocious the noise level in the bar continued to grow as everyone tried to drown him out.

Too loud to carry on a conversation with Pete, I sipped on my beer and waited for the song to end. That is until someone tapped me on the shoulder.

"Hi, Sarah!" It was Cindy Evans and someone I'd never seen before. "We decided to come over the pass and check out open mic night," she shouted.

"We?"

"This is Archie." She pulled the man standing behind her in closer. He was dressed in cargo pants and a dark tank top under an unbuttoned floral shirt. "Archie, this is Sarah."

"G'day Miss," he said, touching the brim of the ball cap he had pulled down over his eyes. "Name's Archie Duncan." He stroked his reddish beard before leaning toward Cindy. "Grab me a pint Love, and I'll find us a spot by the billiard table."

As he wandered off, Cindy put her mouth up to my ear. "Isn't he adorable? And his accent just makes me melt."

"Australian?" I asked.

"Nope," she said, shaking her head. "I thought so too, but he's from New Zealand." She ordered a couple of drafts from Pete as he passed by. "Come to the office Monday. I'll take you to lunch and fill you in." Then she grabbed the beers and disappeared into the crowd.

As I waited for the Kenny Rogers wanna-be to finish, Shellie answered the phone and motioned to Pete that it was for him. After handing him the receiver, she came over.

"Can I get you another beer?"

I shook my head. "I'm good for now."

She leaned on her side of the bar as if waiting for something. As soon as the song was over and the meager applause died down, she leaned closer. "Do you know that man over there?" She pointed toward the pool table at the back of the saloon where Archie was standing behind Cindy and reaching around her, obviously giving her instructions on the finer points of the game. Not that she needed any. She'd beaten me four games out of five the last time we played at her cousin's bar in Alturas, and I'm not exactly a novice pool player.

"The guy in the hat?" I asked.

"Yes, that's him."

"Just met him a few minutes ago. Why?"

"Well," she began, "it's his aura. It's so dark — almost black, really — with a dirty gray overlay."

Having no idea what that meant, I questioned her further. "Is that bad?"

"By itself, not so much. It's the deep red flashes that I'm concerned about." Shaking her head, she shrugged her shoulders and returned to the other end of the bar.

Good grief! But before I could give it another thought, Pete slammed down the receiver and stomped over. "Man, I can't catch a break!"

"What's wrong?" The intensity of his crystal-blue eyes surprised me.

"My buddy can't tow my racing trailer tomorrow. That really bites it because I've already paid my entry fee, and it's non-refundable."

"You can't tow it?" A break in the singing gave us a chance to have an actual conversation.

"Don't have a vehicle capable. Besides, he's also my pit crew. Gotta have somebody help me check the bike and refuel between loops." He cleared the empties and swiped at the top of the bar with a towel. "Too bad we couldn't hook up the trailer to your patrol unit."

"No, can't do that. But..." I polished off my beer. Not sure what I was getting myself into I continued, "...my Dooley should work."

"You have a Dooley?" His wide-eyed expression was quite comical.

"Yes, but I'm not sure how good a pit crew I'd make."

"Shouldn't be too difficult. We just gave the bike a thorough tune-up a few days ago. You'd most likely be filling it with gas while I check the oil and lube the chain."

"I think I can handle that. What time do we leave?"

Before Pete had a chance to answer, the next performer began beating out a solo on the set of drums, completely drowning him out. Smiling, he shrugged and held up four fingers.

"Four in the morning?" That meant I'd have to leave my place no later than 3:15 a.m. Checking my watch, I hoped it wasn't too late. I held up my right index finger, slipped off my barstool, and headed for the door, which proved more challenging than I expected, given the number of patrons squeezed into the place. Once outside, I punched a number into my cell and waited.

"Hello Remy, it's Sarah," I said when he finally answered.

"Hey partner! What's going on? Need some backup?"

"No, no, nothing like that. I was just calling to ask a favor."

"Oh." His voice dripped with disappointment.

"Pete's got a motocross race tomorrow, and I've volunteered to tow his trailer."

"Uh-huh."

"Would you mind watching Bubbles? We have to leave kind of early, and I'm not sure what time we'll be back."

"Sure thing, just bring the little tike by."

"Thanks, Remy. I really appreciate it." I hit the end button and started back inside, but as I reached for the door, it burst open and Cindy and Archie rushed out, holding onto one another and laughing hysterically.

"Sarah!" She stopped and gave me a hug. "I wondered where you'd gone."

"Are you leaving?"

"Yes." She glanced at her date. The man from New Zealand stood a few feet away, his hands in his pockets. "It's too loud and definitely too crowded." Giving me another hug, she whispered, "Don't forget — lunch Monday." Then she linked arms with Archie, and the two of them strolled down the street. As I watched them climb into Cindy's Chevy Impala, I couldn't help wondering who the guy was and how he'd ended up in Modoc County. *And why does he seem so damned familiar?*

By the time I got back to the bar, my stool was occupied, and I couldn't locate Pete anywhere. Shellie was still moving along the mahogany bar quickly mixing drinks, uncapping bottles, and filling glasses with amber liquid from the taps, each topped with a perfect head of foam. "Pete's in the supply room and said for me to send you there when you got back," she said as she passed by.

"Okay, thanks." I stepped away from the bar and began working my way through the crowd until I reached the room at the back of the saloon. I opened the door, stepped through and closed it behind me, instantly muffling the clamor of concert and conversation. Deep shelves lined most of the room's perimeter, and a small metal desk covered with the clutter of running the Silver Spur hunkered next to the door.

Pete was loading a hand truck with an assortment

of alcoholic beverages but stopped as soon as he saw me. "There you are. I was afraid you left."

"Not yet. I had to make arrangements for Bubbles."

He frowned for a moment, then smiled and nodded. "Oh yeah, the dog. Have a seat," he said, motioning toward an ancient-looking chair, "and I'll finish loading this." He went back to stacking cases, the muscles in his arms flexing as he moved each box.

"Where are we going tomorrow?" I asked, avoiding the dilapidated chair and perching on a corner of the desk instead.

"High Rock Canyon, Nevada. That's about fifty miles north of Gerlach." He placed the last box on the stack and wheeled the hand truck toward the door.

"Isn't that where Burning Man takes place?" I hopped off the desk and reached for the doorknob, but Pete parked his load so it blocked the door.

"No, that's further east in the Black Rock Desert." As he grasped my outstretched hand, my anticipation heightened. "I think this will be one of my best races yet," he said, slipping his arms around my waist and pulling me closer.

I had to agree, even though I'd never been to a single one.

Chapter 12

Pulling down Pete's driveway, I wasn't surprised to see him standing next to his utility trailer, a gigantic red duffel and black backpack at his feet. He waved, grabbed his gear, and trotted up to the passenger side before I'd come to a complete stop.

"Morning," he said after tossing the duffel in the backseat and depositing the backpack on the floor of the passenger side.

"Doesn't feel like morning to me," I protested. "At least not yet." Not wanting to be late, I'd skipped my usual breakfast of a PopTart and cup of instant coffee.

"Wait 'til we're on the road. I've got something to share with you." He closed the door and hurried around to my side. "Go ahead and back up to the trailer, and I'll hitch it up," he said after I rolled down my window.

I pulled further around the small circular driveway, trying to get into a better position to back into place, but it still took three tries, adjusting my approach ever so slightly one way or the other each time. Even so, we pulled out of Pete's driveway headed for the tail end of Highway 299 just a few minutes past four.

"This is going to be great," he said, removing a couple of long, foil-wrapped packages from his backpack and placing them on the console between us, along with a few napkins. Then he pulled out a pair of identical travel mugs and placed them in the cup holders mounted in the center of the dash. "Breakfast burritos and hot coffee," he said, unrolling one end of the package closest to me and holding it out. The smell of onions and pesto caused my mouth to salivate and my stomach to grumble.

"Looks delicious, but hang onto it for a second." I turned right at the stop sign and headed for Nevada. "Thanks," I said after getting up to speed and shifting into fifth gear. Using my elbows to steer, I proceeded to devour the burrito and had washed it down with most of my coffee by the time we reached the end of the paved road a few minutes later. "That was amazing," I said, crumpling the foil into a tight ball. "I'm stuffed."

"Glad you like it. I packed a couple of mega sandwiches too, for later."

Glancing at Pete, I was surprised he'd only eaten a few bites of his own burrito. "So how far away is this place we're going to?" I asked, hoping he wouldn't notice how quickly I'd eaten mine.

"Not quite seventy miles," Pete said between sips of coffee.

"Then we should be there in just over an hour." *Why'd we leave so early?*

A mouth full of burrito, he shook his head. "More like two and a half hours," he said after swallowing.

"Two and a half hours!" I downshifted as we climbed out of the valley toward the high plateau of the Nevada desert. "How can it possibly take that long?"

"Narrow dirt road all the way, with lots of twists and turns, but that'll give us lots of time to get to know one another," he said, flashing his big grin at me.

"More than enough time," I agreed. "Why don't you go first?"

"Oh not so fast. Let's make a game of it." He finished off his burrito, gathered up the garbage and stuffed it into his backpack and then tucked the unused napkins in my glove compartment. "Now, you tell me one thing you know about me, and I'll add to it."

Sounds easy enough. "Okay. Well, I know you like to race dirt bikes."

"Gee, ya think?" He chuckled. "Yes I enjoy going on dirt trails very fast. First started racing on BMX bikes when I was five. Then moved up to dirt bikes around the age of eleven and been racing them ever since." He shifted in his seat and rested his left ankle on his right knee. "My turn. You like riding horses."

"Uh, yes I do. Used to compete in rodeos in high school. Started competing in endurance racing when I was living back east."

"Oh new information! Where did you live and for how long?"

"Virginia and a little over seven years. You're from Kentucky, right?" I asked, quickly changing the subject.

Pete nodded.

"So what brought you out west?"

"A strong aversion to becoming a man of the cloth and a wild love of music."

I laughed. "Okay, I get the music part. That's why you're in a band but explain that man of the cloth thing."

He sighed. "Remember I said my dad was a snake handler in the Pentecostal Church?"

I nodded.

"Well, he wanted me to follow in his footsteps and become a preacher. I actually considered it for a while." He shook his head and shifted in his seat again. "But I decided music was more important, so after two years of community college, I headed for LA."

"How did you end up here?"

"Caught a ride with a truck driver who was headed for California. What I didn't know was that he was just passing through the northeastern corner of it. I fell asleep as we were crossing into Nevada, and if he hadn't stopped to take a piss in Alturas, I'd have missed it altogether."

As the road leveled out, it also narrowed. That, and loose gravel, held me to a top speed of thirty-five. "So you never made it to Los Angeles?"

"Nope. Needed cash so I got a job working for a rancher in Cedarville, and I liked the area so much I decided to stay. My folks weren't happy with me but when my younger brother became a preacher, it kinda took the pressure off me."

"What about your sister?"

"Oh she married a horse breeder, so now she has all kinds of horses to ride and lots of people to chase after them when she falls off."

I turned to glare at him but his wink made me laugh instead. "Well, I bet no one captures her horse with as much flair as you."

"You're probably right." He shifted in his seat again, and we rode in silence for a few miles. "Damn coffee," he said finally. "Time for a pit stop."

I engaged on the clutch and eased the Dooley to a stop. Pete jumped out and took a few steps from the open door. As he relieved himself, I looked around in the dim light of predawn for a spot where I could do the same. However, what few sagebrush I could see did not offer the kind of privacy I required, so I decided to wait, hoping for more adequate cover further down the road.

"Okay, my turn," Pete said, climbing back in. He buckled up and made himself comfortable. "I'm assuming you lived in Virginia when you were in the FBI."

"How did you know — Remy! What else did he tell you?"

"Just that you moved back to California when you got the job as deputy sheriff. So what made you give up a career in the Federal Bureau of Investigation? It had to have been way more exciting than being a deputy in Surprise Valley."

I didn't answer right away but stared straight ahead, thinking about what to say. "The change in career is a long story that I don't want to talk about now. I will tell you I like my job, and I like living in Surprise Valley."

"Fair enough. Now tell me about your family. I know you have one sister that owns a dog."

"Alexis, and she's almost more annoying than I can stand. No other siblings, and both my parents are retired and living in Red Bluff."

"Must be nice having your family so close. Sometimes I really miss seeing my folks, especially around the holidays. Makes having friends like Shellie all that more important, if you know what I mean."

I did. Sue James and I spent every holiday together since we'd met, and living in the same apartment complex in Virginia eliminated any loneliness I might have felt. Funny thing was, I hadn't seen my parents any more frequently than when I was living on the other side of the country, and I think we all preferred it that way. "I agree. Without Cindy — you met her the other night — and Scott Jenkins — a fellow deputy I went to high school with — this would be a very lonely place. And, of course, there's Remy too."

"Yeah, he's a funny old guy, isn't he? He comes to the bar at least twice a week to hang out and have a scotch or two. If I didn't know better, I'd think he has a thing for Shellie."

"Really?" It made sense that he might be looking for a companion, but the way he always spoke of his deceased wife, Peggy, I'd never considered it a possibility. *Good for you, Remy!* "Does Shellie suspect anything?"

"If she does, she hasn't let on — Watch it!!" he shouted pointing to the left side of the dirt road.

Practically standing on the brake, I brought the Dooley and trailer to a lurching halt just as a huge doe dashed across the road, barely missing the front bumper.

"Wow, that was close!" Pete said as he released his grip on the dashboard in front of him.

"Yeah," I agreed. My hands were shaking, and the slight need to use the bathroom was suddenly urgent.

"Where are you going?" he asked as I shut off the motor and climbed out the truck.

"Nature calls." I started toward the biggest sagebrush I could find. "And no peeking," I called over my shoulder.

"Scout's honor."

I doubted Pete had been a boy scout, but I had to take my chances. Feeling much relieved a few minutes later, we were again on our way, bathed in the warmth of the rising sun.

The desert plateau looked like the parking lot of a gigantic trailer dealership. Utility trailers of all sizes hitched to vehicles ranging from dilapidated pickups to state-of-the-art recreational vehicles were parked in several long rows. The smell of high octane fuel permeated the cab as I passed racing teams working on their bikes, the sound of their engines vibrating against the rigs.

"Pull in over there," Pete said, pointing to the right. "This'll be a good central location and easy access between loops."

Slowly, I guided my truck alongside a black and tan diesel pusher and matching trailer at least twice the size of Pete's that probably cost more than my house and five acres in Fort Bidwell.

"Before we unload my bike, I need to check in." Pete grabbed a large manila envelope from his backpack and set off for a huge white tent in the center of the parking area. As I chased after him, the excitement of anticipation charged the chilly air like electricity. It was a familiar feeling from my own endurance competitions, and I was surprised at how much I missed it.

Similar to a circus tent with tarps for a floor, one section had a row of tables where riders were checking in, and Pete headed for it right away. Another area held a complete snack bar, which included tables and chairs and an island of soda machines. A first aid station with a separate entrance ran along the back of the tent. The rest of the tent was taken up by clusters of folding chairs. Most interesting was the strategic placement of huge fans along opposing sides of the structure. I was about to question someone wearing a blaze orange vest with NHHA printed on the back when Pete came up behind me.

"Pretty crazy, huh?"

"Yeah." I said, following him to the main entrance. "What does NHHA stand for?" I asked, pointing at an official as he hurried by.

"National Hare and Hound Association."

"Hare and hound?"

"It's just what they call this kind of race. The riders in front are considered the hares and the rest, who are trying to catch them, are the hounds."

"I see." We stepped outside into the bright morning, and I wished I'd grabbed my sunglasses. "And what are those fans for?"

"When the temperature goes up, they fire up a generator so the fans can keep the air moving through the tent. Otherwise it gets really hot in here."

"How hot?"

"Well over a hundred. Come on, I want to show you something." He led me over to a raised platform about twenty feet off the ground, and we climbed to the top. "You see that truck parked way over there?"

he asked, pointing to an old blue Chevy truck that looked like one my dad used to own.

"Yeah."

"That's the banner truck. They hold up this huge red banner in the bed of it and when it drops, the race starts. The starting line is over there," he pointed to the west, "and the trail begins about a mile in that direction." He pointed somewhere to the east, but all I could see were miles of scattered sagebrush. Standing closer, he wrapped one arm around my waist. "I'm so glad you came," he said, looking down at me. My pulse quickened at his touch, but before I could relax into his embrace, he dropped his arm and stepped back. "Now, let's go get my bike ready."

Chapter 13

Still trying to recover from his brief display of affection, I followed Pete down the ladder and back to his trailer, dodging dirt bikes as they zipped back and forth, their riders working out any last minute bugs. He unlocked the side door first and wrestled out some kind of rubber mat. Unrolled, it covered a ten-by-ten square of ground at the back of the trailer. Then he opened and lowered the back door, which created a ramp running from the trailer to the mat. Together we removed the restraints from his Kawasaki 450 and rolled it out. "Hang onto it while I grab the stand." He disappeared into the trailer and, after a lot of clanking and banging, returned carrying something that resembled a footstool with a handle. After he got it into position, we hefted the bike onto it.

"Do we need to tie it down?" I asked, not sure if I should let go.

"Nope. The platform on top has a non-skid surface. See?" He gently clasped my hands and pulled them off the handle bar. "It balances here just fine. Now we'll unload my tools."

Ten minutes later we had his tool box rolled out and opened up and two folding chairs and a giant ice chest placed in a tiny patch of shade. I grabbed a bottle of water, sat in one of the chairs, and watched Pete make some kind of an adjustment to the chain. Next he checked the air pressure in the tires as well as the cables I assumed operated the brakes and clutch. "Okay, let's see how this thing runs."

We tugged it off the stand, and he got on, fired it up, and rode off. Every now and then I'd catch a glimpse of him as he maneuvered up and down the rows of parked vehicles. Finally he came back, an enormous smile on his face.

"This bike has never sounded so good," he said, cutting the engine. "I'll get the rest of the gear ready, give you the rundown on what you'll need to do between loops, and then I'll get changed." By the time he stepped into the trailer with his red duffel bag, we had the gas cans lined up, goggles cleaner and lubricating oil ready, his custom-made pack loaded with four bottles of water and the zippered compartment stuffed with a handful of jerky and an apple. With a vague notion of what I'd have to do between loops, I'd settled into one of the chairs and was waiting for Pete.

Switching outfits faster than a runway model, he emerged from the trailer, dressed in a black and white racing jersey, which had streaks of red and yellow and the Rockstar energy drink emblem across his chest.

"I didn't know you had a sponsor," I said, holding his pack in place so he could fasten the strap.

"I don't, but if I keep wearing their gear and finishing in the top five I might." He pulled on his helmet, slid his hands into his gloves, and one more time we lifted his bike off the stand. "I have to go to the mandatory riders' meeting at the starting line," he said, his voice muffled. "You might get a spot on the platform if you head over now. At least you can see the start of the race from there, and I should be back in a couple of hours, if not sooner." He straddled the bike, started the engine and revved it a couple of times.

"I'll be ready," I yelled. "Good luck." I stepped back, and he pulled away slowly for the first fifty feet. Then he gunned it and sped off toward the starting line. Reaching into the cab of my truck, I grabbed my sunglasses and the binoculars I'd thrown in last minute. Then, after fishing another bottle of water out of the ice chest, I headed for the raised platform.

I found a spot in one of the front corners and braced myself against the railing. Pushing my sunglasses up on my head, I peered through the binoculars, scanning the growing crowd of riders for Pete. I spotted at least eight possibilities but couldn't make a positive identification, so I gave up, deciding to enjoy the action as it unfolded.

Racing officials in their orange vests scurried back and forth, speaking into their walkie-talkies as they went. Several of them headed toward the old Chevy truck Pete had pointed out and within a few minutes had the banner in place. The riders were getting ready as well, dispersing themselves along the starting line, which seemed to stretch for over a quarter of a mile.

All of a sudden, the drone from their engines that had become part of the background ceased, and an eerie silence settled over the area. Conversations, if they continued, were reduced to whispers, and everyone's attention was drawn to the riders. Seconds ticked by as the anticipation grew, until finally the banner wavered and then fell.

Engines fired and bikes lurched forward. As the riders sped toward the trail entrance, a cloud of dust began to build; so thick, it obscured everything in its path as it swept across the desert floor. Finally, a few dirt bikes managed to break free and move ahead of the rest. Maneuvering closer together, one rider accelerated and took the lead. Partially hidden by his own dust cloud, it was difficult to see the color of his jersey and therefore identify the rider; that is, until he entered the trail. Veering to the right, he flew up a small rise and sailed over a large sagebrush. That's when I knew; Pete was the hare!

The first hour went by quickly. I'd stayed on the platform until the last dirt bike made it to the trail. When the huge dust cloud dissipated, however, it became clear that not everyone made it that far. Three bikes had collided just off the starting line, and officials were trying to keep the riders from pummeling each other. The front wheel of another bike had come off and that rider was just getting to his feet. Two other bikes were being pushed back to the parking area for reasons not yet disclosed.

After climbing down, I reentered the tent, bought myself a diet Pepsi, and wandered over to the registration area to check out the race course on the big maps they had hanging on the wall. The first loop of the race was a gigantic circle that meandered through the sagebrush scattered about the flat floor of the desert. The second loop veered off to the right and looked more like a maze as it crisscrossed through the mountainous region to the east, following creek beds and climbing up and over peaks. Hanging alongside the maps were pictures taken along the trail, one showing the trail running along the top of a narrow ridge that I would find frightening to walk along let alone navigate on a dirt bike at high speed.

Still sipping my soda, I strolled up and down the rows of rigs, observing how other pit crews spent their time waiting. On my second pass, I came upon one of the dirt bikes that had been forced to drop out of the race. Its pieces were spread out on a mat similar to Pete's and a guy in his twenties was sorting parts and wiping his greasy hands on his grey tank top. Wearing a dirty ball cap jammed onto his frizzy red hair, he looked up as I walked by, and judging by the black eye and a bloody tissue rolled up and stuck in one nostril, I assumed he was one of the brawling trio that had crashed.

Continuing my stroll, I noticed most of the teams were sitting around talking. Some were reading magazines and others appeared to by napping, which seemed like a good idea considering how early I'd gotten up. Without wasting another minute, I cut across the remaining rows of vehicles and headed straight for Pete's trailer. A few moments later, I was settled in one of the chairs, my feet propped up on the ice chest. With a fresh bottle of water and selected reading material at my fingertips, I closed my eyes and drifted off to sleep.

A mosquito. Buzzing toward me, getting louder and louder, but I can't see it. Where is it coming from? Too loud, too close! Then nothing.

"Hey, Sleeping Beauty! Nap time's over!"

Startled awake, I was surprised to see Pete standing next to his dirt bike. I jumped out of my chair and helped him get it on the stand. While he pulled off his helmet and gloves, I fueled it, emptying one full can of gas and part of another into the tank. Then he lubed the chain and checked the cables, as I reloaded his water pack and retrieved one of the huge sandwiches he'd packed.

"I didn't expect you back so soon," I said, watching him devour at least half of it as ravenously as I'd dispatched my breakfast burrito.

"Me neither," he managed around the mouthful of food. "But that run was amazing. It was like I was part of the bike. Never hesitated, no sliding, just ran balls out the whole way." He flashed that huge grin of his, and I couldn't help but smile back. I'd often felt the exact same way riding Raven.

"Okay, time to hit the trail again," he said, wrapping his sandwich up and thrusting it at me.

As I helped him pull the dirt bike off the stand, the droning of distant engines materialized, growing louder with each passing second. "Are you in first place?" I asked, the realization suddenly hitting me.

Again the big grin. "Yup and I plan on keeping it that way!" He swung his leg over, and I held out his helmet and gloves. As he took hold of them, he pulled me in closer and kissed me hard on the lips. "For luck!" Then he crammed his helmet on his head, tugged on his gloves, and roared off. Within seconds, more dirt bikes poured in, zigzagging as they went, each looking for the quickest way to its support vehicle.

As I put away what was left of Pete's sandwich, I thought about digging out mine but decided I wasn't hungry enough to really enjoy it. Instead, I put away tools and gas cans and went in search of a way to kill a couple of hours.

"Here they come!" someone on the raised platform yelled as I walked by. It was the third trip I'd made to the huge tent as a means of passing the time. Instead of continuing on my way, I did an abrupt about-face, sprinted back to the truck to grab my binoculars, and went in search of a vantage point. Fortunately, I reached the raised platform well before everyone else, so I scaled the ladder and began scanning for riders.

More than a mile out, I spotted a single plume of dust kicked up by the lead rider. *Is Pete still the hare?* Several hundred yards behind him, a much larger dust cloud revealed the hounds in swift pursuit. Minutes ticked by as the competitors sped toward the finish line. Anxiously I watched the lone dust plume, hoping to catch a glimpse of the rider. Finally he cleared the rock formations that hindered my view and, although not positive, I was fairly certain it was Pete. *YES!*

I scrambled down the ladder, careful not to lose my footing, and headed for the finish line, my binoculars bouncing as I ran. Within seconds of reaching the crowd that had already gathered, Pete flew across the imaginary line and slid to a stop.

As I hurried over to congratulate him, he ripped the helmet off his head and threw it to the ground. "Goddam stupid son-of-a-bitch!" He bailed off his bike, dumping it in the dirt before I could get there to hold it. "I'm gonna pound that guy as soon as I lay eyes on him." He started back toward the finish line.

"Pete," I called, trying to catch up to him. "What the hell is going on?"

"Some guy in a neon green jersey rammed into me as we were crossing a really narrow ridge. Practically shoved me over the edge." I had a pretty good idea which place Pete was talking about.

As soon as we reached the finish line, he started pacing back and forth while he waited for the next group of riders to come in. A small group of five or six dirt bikes came in, but none of them wore a neon green jersey. A few moments later, another group of riders finished the race but still no neon green. Group after group crossed the finish line, Pete scrutinizing each rider but not finding the one he was looking for. "This is bullshit!" Without another word, he sprinted back to his bike, retrieved his helmet and jammed it on his head. Then he jerked his bike off the ground, straddled it and roared off, heading back the way he'd come and throwing a huge rooster tail of sand behind him.

"Pete!" I yelled as he sped past me, but he didn't even slow down. *Good grief!* Not knowing what else to do, I stood with my arms crossed over my chest and watched him disappear from my view.

Chapter 14

As I headed back to the trailer, a voice came over the PA system. "Pete Yarbrough, please report to the registration desk."

I almost ignored the announcement but then thought better of it. I pushed my way through the crowd that had gathered outside the tent and made my way to the table where Pete had signed in earlier that day. "He's not here right now," I told the bald man with a rather large gut seated behind it.

"Sorry?"

"Pete Yarbrough. He's not here right now. He took off back up the trail, looking for a rider that had run into him on the course."

"Well, have him report in as soon as he gets back. He needs to sign for his winnings," the man said.

"Will do." As I left the tent, the smell of roasting hot dogs made my stomach growl. "Time to have my sandwich," I said as I pushed back through the crowd and strolled to the trailer.

Forty minutes later, I'd polished off my sandwich and washed it down with a bottle of water, and still no sign of Pete. Thinking he might have returned but not come back to the trailer, I headed for the tent. The crowd had thinned a little, making it easier to get inside. The same big-bellied man was still sitting at the table. "Excuse me," I began, "did Pete Yarbrough check in yet?"

"No and I wish he would. I can't get things wrapped up until he collects his prize money. Where did you say he went?"

I again explained about Pete's experience with the rider in a neon green jersey. "Do you think something might have happened out there?" I asked.

"Well, first I'll check to see if we have any riders unaccounted for." He heaved his body out of the chair and moved down the table to where a tiny woman with dark hair wound into a bun was making marks on a large paper grid. "Hey Shirley, we got any riders unaccounted for?"

"Hang on Bud, I got four more finish times to enter and then I can tell you." She continued to flip through the small pieces of paper in her hand and make marks on the grid. "Yeah, looks like we got one that hasn't come in. Vince Dixon."

"Got it." Bud waddled back to his place at the table and picked up the microphone that was sitting there. "Vince Dixon or someone from his racing team please report to the registration desk." He placed the microphone back on the table. "Now, we'll just see who shows up." He eased himself back into his chair, and we waited. Minutes ticked by until a young boy of about ten with tousled blond hair skidded to a stop in front of the table.

"You looking for Vince?" he asked.

"That's right." Bud shifted in his chair. "He back yet?"

"We ain't seen no sign of him. We just figured

he'd had some kinda trouble and was pushing his bike in."

"Okay then," Bud said. "You come back and let us know when he shows up."

"Sure thing."

As the kid turned to go, I reached out and put my hand on his shoulder. "What color jersey is Vince wearing?"

"Bright green."

I looked at Bud. "Okay thanks," I said, removing my hand. As soon as he was out of earshot I continued. "We may have a problem."

"Whaddya mean?"

"I mean that sounds like the guy Pete went to find. And if he found him..." *If he found him, what?* I had no idea what Pete was capable of, and I'd never seen him that mad. Not even when his Harley had been stolen or his bar damaged by a stool-throwing drunk.

"You may have a point. I'll send Shorty out in the Ranger to look for them."

"I'd like to go too, if that's okay."

"Well..." He scratched his head just above the receding hairline. "Guess there's no harm in letting you tag along." He pulled the radio off his belt. "Shorty, grab your Ranger and meet me at the front entrance of the tent."

"Copy that," the radio crackled.

By the time Bud and I exited the tent, the Ranger and its driver were waiting. True to his nickname, Shorty sat toward the front edge of his seat, so his feet could reach the pedals.

"We've got a couple missing riders," Bud said, as I walked around and slid into the passenger seat.

"This here gal's gonna ride out with you to look for them."

Shorty turned to me, a big grin on his face. "Howdy. Name's Shorty," he said, offering his right hand.

"Sarah," I said, giving his hand a firm shake.

He turned back to Bud. "I'll radio ya if we find anything." Then, without another word, he stomped on the accelerator, and we took off for the start of the second loop. Reaching the narrow trail, Shorty took it at full speed, bouncing the Ranger over rocks and small bushes hard enough to raise his butt off the seat. Bracing my feet against the dash and gripping the roll bar with both hands was the only thing that kept me from being pitched out of the ATV. He slowed down a little as we began to climb a rock-studded knoll but not enough to convince me to loosen my grip. Almost to the top, the trail veered to the right and wound around just below the peak. It was here that Shorty finally slowed way down, and I could relax my tense muscles.

"Right along in here the trail gets real tricky for the next couple of miles," Shorty began. "Drops-offs and narrow places with loose gravel can really mess with a rider if he ain't paying attention."

Halfway around the knoll, the trail veered right again and ran along the top of a ridge so narrow, there were only two or three feet between the edge of the precipice and the Ranger. I instantly recognized it as the section of the trail I'd seen in a photo hanging inside the tent. What hadn't been in the shot was the dirt bike lying on its side that now blocked the trail.

"That's Pete's bike," I said, pointing ahead of us,

"and that's his helmet." Shorty brought the Ranger to within a few feet of them and cut the engine.

I bailed out, careful not to get too close to the edge, and ran over to check the bike. "Doesn't look like it crashed but rather was laid on its side." I cupped my hands around my mouth. "Pete! Where are you? Pete!"

"Here, down here!" a voice answered.

Shorty and I exchanged glances and immediately began walking along the edge of the trail, one on each side. Jagged rocks formed make-shift ledges, some barely big enough to stand on. *No wonder Pete was so pissed off!*

"Got 'em," Shorty yelled, and I ran over to where he was standing. Peering over the edge, I was shocked to find Pete crouched over the motionless body of a rider in a neon green jersey. While slightly bigger than most of the ledges I'd seen, it barely had enough room for the rider's torso let along someone else.

"Are you okay?" I called.

"I'm fine, but we need to get this guy out of here. He keeps slipping in and out of consciousness. I think he's hurt pretty bad."

"I'll get on the horn and get the medics out here pronto," Shorty said, heading back to the Ranger.

"How did you get down there?" I asked Pete, looking for a way down.

"Not sure," he replied. "Mostly, I just slid down on my ass and hoped for the best."

"So where's his bike?" I asked.

"I'm guessing down there somewhere." Pete pointed over his shoulder with his thumb.

Looking through my binoculars, which I still

wore around my neck, I spotted it at the base of the ravine, badly mangled and probably irretrievable. "Yeah, I see it, or what's left of it."

"They're on the way," Shorty called as he scurried back along the trail. "I need to back out of here, turn around and then drive back this way in reverse. We'll probably need to use the winch on the front to help pull the guy up. Can you push this bike further along the trail? That's about where I'll need to park."

"Sure." I leaned over the edge. "Be right back." Then, as I stood up Pete's bike and wheeled it out of the way, Shorty fired up the ATV and began backing it off the narrow trail until he found a place wide enough to turn around. Watching him back toward me was nerve-racking, especially when his tires crept dangerously close to either edge before he realized it and changed direction. By the time he got the vehicle into position and climbed out, I heard engines in the distance.

I walked back to where Pete clung to the side of the cliff. He was standing and rubbing his right leg. As I squeezed by the Ranger, I'd noticed a coil of Safeline in the back. "Do you want help getting back up to the trail?" I called.

"Thanks, but I'll wait until the rescue team arrives. Don't want him thrashing about and pitching himself over the edge."

"Won't be long now. I can hear them coming." Looking through my binoculars again, I focused on where the trail disappeared as it wound around the adjacent hilltop. Little by little the drone of the approaching vehicle grew in intensity until finally, I detected movement as a quad rounded the corner.

"Here they come," Shorty shouted from the

position he'd taken several yards up the trail. "Looks like they sent the whole crew. Time to get the show on the road." He trotted back to the Ranger and began fiddling with the winch.

The quad, loaded down with two riders and a Stokes litter across the front, was followed by a dirt bike also hauling two riders. It definitely was a rescue squad. I wanted to feel relieved but experience told me the real challenge was still ahead — getting the injured man back up to the trail without losing anyone over the edge. My stomach clenched. This wasn't going to be easy.

"Okay, hoist me up," Pete called when he had the harness secured. One of the medics, his safety line tied to the Ranger, had climbed down to take Pete's place with the rider in the neon green jersey, and now Pete was being pulled to safety. My heart beat faster as each foot of cable wound onto the quad's winch. Relief finally came when his head popped above the edge of the trail. Reaching down, I grabbed one of his hands and helped him to his feet.

"Let's get you out of this," Shorty said, stepping in and pushing me aside. He unbuckled Pete's harness, disconnected it from the cable, and tossed it to the other medic, who was then tied off to the quad and lowered over the edge within minutes.

"Now, as soon as the guy is in," Shorty began, grabbing both controllers as the remaining two members of the rescue squad hooked each of the winch cables to the litter, "you'll need to help haul them two up so I can work the winches." Standing spraddle-legged between the quad and the Ranger, a controller in each hand like a gunslinger ready for a shootout, he began letting out the cables as the litter was carried to the edge and sent it over the side. Pete and I watched as it inched closer and closer to the waiting medics.

"That's good!" one of the medics called as soon as it was in position. Quickly, they maneuvered the backboard under the injured man and slid him toward the litter. Wanting to be ready to haul them up, Pete and I moved toward the quad. But before we reached it, the front end lurched toward the edge and yells of surprise rose from below. We threw ourselves at it in an attempt to hold it in place. At the same time we grabbed the rope connected to the medic dangling below.

"Here we go!" Shorty hollered. As the winches worked in tandem raising the litter, the four of us pulled on the ropes with all our might, hauling the rescuers to safety. Progress was slow, and by the time everyone was back on the trail, my shoulders ached and my arms were shaking.

"Let's get him loaded," Shorty directed as soon as the cables were detached. While the rest of us secured the litter on the back of the Ranger, he finished winding the cables onto each winch and disconnected the controllers. "Now, you fellas get your gear. We need to get this guy back a.s.a.p."

Pete and I stood out of the way as the medics grabbed their kits and started working, one crouching next to the rider and the other kneeling in the passenger seat. The other two guys jumped on the quad and dirt bike that had brought them out on the trail, fired them up, and started back the way they'd come.

"Uh, I'm afraid there's no room for you on the

Ranger," Shorty said as he approached us. "Guess I should've had one of them guys haul you back."

"That's all right." Pete wrapped his arm around my waist. "She can ride back with me, only I might not have enough gas to make it."

"That's an easy fix." Shorty scampered back to the Ranger, grabbed a small gas can from under the litter and hustled back. "This should be more than enough," he said, holding it out.

"Thanks," Pete said, taking the can. "Give me a hand?"

I nodded, and together we stood up his bike and topped off the tank. As soon as Pete returned the empty can to Shorty, the anxious driver started the Ranger and headed back, considerably slower than when I rode out with him.

Pete picked up his helmet and tried to put it on my head, but I held up my hand and stopped him. "What the hell were you doing riding back out here?"

He flashed his huge smile, blue eyes twinkling, and shrugged. "I was just so damn mad, I had to do something."

"Well, you had me worried."

"I did?" He leaned closer to me.

"Oh stop it!" I placed my hand on his chest and pushed him away. "You rode off without a word and then got yourself into a situation you couldn't get out of. What were you thinking sliding down to that ledge with no way to get help?"

His smile faded and his blue eyes deepened. "I just knew."

"Knew what?"

He again leaned closer, wrapped his arms around me, and kissed me. When we parted, he brushed a hunk of hair out of my face and said, "That you'd come looking for me."

"Oh you knew that, did you?"

He smiled and nodded. "Come on, let's get going." He slid the helmet over my head. "I've got winnings to collect."

Chapter 15

Waking with arms of rubber and excruciating pain in my shoulders was not a good way to start the week. A tearing sensation between my shoulder blades when I brushed my teeth told me braiding my hair was out of the question. I did manage to comb out the ends and flip it over my shoulders so it hung down my back. After swallowing four ibuprofen tablets, putting on my uniform was slightly easier, and by the time I was ready to go, my muscles seemed to have loosened up a little.

I eased into Remy's driveway and opened my door, but before I could release my seatbelt and get out, Bubbles leapt across me, ran up on the deck and scratched at the front door. Moments later, it opened, a hand waved at me and then the door closed. Chuckling to myself, I pulled down the dirt road and onto the pavement, headed for Cedarville. I'd just passed Lake City when my cell phone went off.

"Deputy Murdock."

"Deputy, this is Lulu DeLoure. I work for the *Alturas Gazette,* and I recently learned of a rash of livestock thefts in the Eagleville area. Is it true that you have no idea how these animals are being taken?"

I pulled over immediately. "Miss DeLoure..."

"Oh please, call me Lulu," she interjected.

"Miss DeLoure, I wouldn't call two missing alpacas a rash of livestock thefts. And while there doesn't seem to be any evidence, it is an ongoing investigation."

"I see. Well, I'm writing a piece about this for next week's paper and would like to meet with you to compare notes; uh, I mean discuss your progress."

I involuntarily rolled my eyes and shook my head. "I'll be in Alturas later today if that works for you; although, I'm not sure I'll be able to provide you with any more information than you already have."

"That'll be great! Uh, I mean..." She paused briefly. "That's a good time for me. You can reach me at this number, and I look forward to meeting you." Then she hung up. Not sure what to make of the phone call, I pulled back onto County Road 1 and continued my patrol.

By 10:00, I'd crested the summit of Cedar Pass and was coasting down the other side toward Alturas. I needed to see the lab tech; it had been a week and I still hadn't heard anything about the cloth bag or wooden box I'd found in the victim's truck. That wasn't like Josh, but maybe he'd gotten swamped.

I pulled into the parking lot, entered the back door of the offloading room, and crossed the hall into the lab. Josh was perched on a stool and peering into a microscope.

"Hey Sarah," he said when he noticed me. "Don't tell me you've got another 11-44 to deliver."

"Not today," I said, shaking my head. "Actually I was wondering if you'd finished processing that box and bag from the truck we recovered."

"Days ago. You didn't get a copy of my report?"

I shook my head again.

"Damn it." Josh untangled his long legs from the stool, and stepped over to his desk. "He said he'd forward it to you. Should've just done it myself." He adjusted his heavy-framed glasses and began rummaging through the papers on his desk

"Who said?"

"Sandusky."

No wonder they call him Dirk the Jerk! "Oh. No, I haven't gotten a thing."

"Here." Josh handed me a hard copy of his report. "Sorry you didn't get it sooner."

I pushed my sunglasses up on my head and flipped through the pages. "So nothing out of the ordinary, huh?"

"Not really." He headed back toward his work table but stopped. Turning back to me he continued, "There was the faint hint of some kind of odor. Kinda musky, but I couldn't put my finger on it." He shrugged and went back to his microscope.

"Thanks." I folded the report and slipped it into my back pocket. Curious, I returned to the offloading room where the bigger evidence items were stored. I found the wooden box on a lower shelf and picked up the bag, which had been folded neatly and placed on top. Holding it to my nose, I breathed in. The smell was definitely familiar, but I couldn't figure out from when or where. Perplexed, I replaced it and headed for the dispatcher's desk.

Cindy was working on the computer when I leaned on the counter that separated her desk from the public. "Hungry for lunch yet?" I asked.

She swiveled her chair until she was facing me.

"Hey, Sarah! Glad you made it. Give me two seconds to finish this up and I'll be ready."

"Okay." I wandered back the way I'd come and went into the break room. Scott was leaning against the tiny counter devouring something from the vending machine. He waved, nodded and began chewing furiously. Two other deputies were seated at the table in the corner, sharing a huge deli sandwich and a bag of barbecued potato chips.

"Howdy, Sarah!" Scott said when his mouth was finally empty. "Don't see you here too often. Whatcha got goin' on?"

"Nothing exciting. Just going to lunch with Cindy."

"Lunch?" His crooked smiled appeared.

I shook my head. "Sorry — girls only."

His smile vanished. "Oh. I thought maybe we'd get together before I take off."

"Where you going?"

"Sandusky signed me up for some kind of training in Sacramento. I'll be gone for a week."

"When are you leaving?" I settled into the closest chair; Scott did likewise.

"Wednesday."

With things seemingly settled down on my side of the Warners, a night out on the big town of Alturas was a definite possibility. "Sounds good. How about tomorrow?"

Scott leapt out of his chair and the smile reappeared. "Great! Be at Lenny's Bar and Grill around 7:00, and I'll see if I can round up a few of the guys to join us."

Before I could respond, Cindy poked her head around the door jam. "Let's go, girlfriend."

"Coming," Scott said in his most feminine voice, as he wiggle-walked toward her.

Cindy glowered at him and showed him the palm of her hand. "Not funny, Jenkins!" Scott paused mid-wiggle, sporting a pout any toddler would be proud of. "Come on, Sarah," she said, gesturing at me to follow.

Looking back at Scott, I shrugged my shoulders and smiled. He held his right hand up next to his face and gave me a five-fingered wave. *Oh, brother!*

"Let's walk down to Subway," Cindy suggested as we stepped out into the bright sunshine. "I just love their new chopped salads." A meatball sub swimming in marinara was the first thing that came to **my** mind.

"Okay. Sounds good," I said, lowering my sunglasses into place.

We'd barely gotten our food and found a place to sit down when Cindy, not able to contain herself any longer, started in. "Last week began like any other; that is, until Tuesday. I'm sitting in the park, eating my lunch as usual, when this guy on a motorcycle pulls up." Her eyes brightened. "Right away, I could tell he wasn't from Alturas.

"Anyway, he comes over to where I'm sitting, carrying a small grocery bag and a tattered paperback, and asks with that dreamy accent of his if he can join me." She paused and took a deep breath. "All I could do was nod my head. I must've looked like a gawky schoolgirl.

"Anyhow, he pulls an apple out of the bag, opens his book and starts reading." She shook her head. "Every time he glanced my way, there I was staring at him. Finally, he closed his book, and we just started talking, like we'd known each other forever." She popped the lid off her salad and started eating.

"That's it?"

"No," Cindy said around her mouthful of food, "but I'm starving." She swallowed and continued. "Apparently, Archie was teaching middle school somewhere back east but got laid off, so he decided to travel around on his motorcycle and see the rest of the country before going back home to New Zealand. Isn't that romantic?"

"How did he end up here? Alturas isn't exactly a tourist attraction." I waited while she ate some more salad.

A few bites later, she continued. "He was on his way north to Oregon and Washington but low on cash, so he stayed here, hoping to find a job and a place to stay."

"Oh." I finished off my sandwich and wadded the paper into a ball. "That may be difficult, being someone that's just passing through."

She shook her head again. "Uncle Bert's been looking for someone to help out at the tire shop, and he's already settled in at the motel — in the exact same room you were in." She smiled, and her eyes got that dreamy, faraway look. "He said that if things work out, he might even stay for a while."

Although I couldn't put my finger on anything specific, something didn't feel right about the whole thing. Perhaps it was my lack of understanding of those who are comfortable roaming from place to place, relying on their wits for something to eat and a place to stay. Maybe it was Shellie's reading of his aura. Then again, maybe it was nothing. "So how many times have you seen this Archie guy?"

"Well, we met on Tuesday, I took him to meet Uncle Bert on Wednesday, had lunch in the park on Thursday and Friday, came to the Spur on Saturday. Oh, and on Sunday he took me for a motorcycle ride, then I cooked him dinner and we watched movies. How many is that?"

"Six. I'm surprised you had room on your calendar for lunch with me."

"Of course I did. Besides he had to help Uncle Bert deliver tires to Tule Lake." She grinned at me, gathered up all the trash, and threw it in the garbage can by the door. Last, she topped off her diet Coke. "Need all the caffeine I can get. I was up kinda late last night."

At that point, I didn't want to hear any more. "Well, I have to get going. Thanks for lunch." But as we started out the door, Cindy's phone chimed.

"Oh, that's Archie." She rummaged around in her purse, almost spilling her drink, until she found it. Slipping into the nearest seat and without looking at me, she said, "I'll talk to you later." So I left her there, smiling and texting.

Rather than calling the reporter, I decided to just stop by the newspaper office before heading back over Cedar Pass. Located on the south end of Main Street, I pulled into the *Gazette*'s tiny parking lot and slipped into the slot closest to the entrance.

As I pushed through the front door, the conversation between two girls that looked to be twenty at the most halted, and they watched me approach the business counter, wide-eyed.

"Uh, can I help you?" the taller one asked.

"I'm looking for Lulu DeLoure."

Without taking her eyes off me, the shorter one

stepped back a couple of steps and called over her shoulder, "Oh Lulu, there's someone here to see you." Moving back closer to me, she whispered, "Is she in some kind of trouble?"

"Not at all," I said, offering my most friendly smile. "She asked if I'd stop by." *Not exactly true, but they'll never know.*

"Can I help..." The woman who rounded the corner did not fit the stereotypical image of a female reporter that I had imagined. This woman appeared six feet tall in the four-inch spikes she wore. And if her clothes didn't make her stand out — short plaid skirt and ruffled white blouse versus the jeans and cap-sleeved T-shirts worn by her co-workers — her hair definitely did. Bleached to a honey-blond color and cropped close to her head, it was adorned with a shock of neon pink right above her forehead that clashed with the red frames of her oversized glasses. "You must be Deputy Murdock," she said, extending her right hand. "I'm Lulu DeLoure."

Returning the gesture and nodding, it took all my effort to focus on her face and not her Muppet hair.

"We can go to the small conference room. Hold all my calls and no interruptions," she commanded the other two.

"Yes, Miss DeLoure," said one.

"Of course, Miss DeLoure," said the other, followed by not-so-subdued giggling.

Lulu stopped by a small desk shoved into an out-of-the-way corner and grabbed a notebook before leading me into a tiny room lined with shelves stuffed to capacity. A card table and two folding chairs sat in the middle.

"Now Deputy," she began, opening her notebook,

"A Mr. Robertson contacted our paper regarding his missing alpacas."

"So, he asked you to write an article about it?" I asked.

"Not exactly." Her face deepened in color, starting at her chin and sweeping upward.

"Then why did he call?"

She cleared her throat. "He wanted to place an ad offering a reward for any information about the missing animals, but I thought it would make a great story."

"What exactly is your job here at the *Gazette*?" I asked.

She looked down at her hands. "Um, I take the calls having to do with the classified ads and type them up."

"Then you're not a reporter?"

"Not yet, but I know I'd be a great one if I only got the chance."

"And how did you get my name and number?"

"Well, after I hung up with Mr. Robertson, I called the Sheriff's Office to find out who was handling the investigation." She flipped a page in her notebook. "A Mr. Sandusky gave me your name and cell phone number, claiming you were on the cutting edge of crime in Modoc County."

Unbelievable! "Okay, so tell me what you've got."

She consulted her notebook again. "Well, two baby alpacas are missing and there is no sign on how they were taken or by whom."

"Yeah, that about sums it up."

"No footprints or hairs or fibers anywhere?" She sounded like Remy, and I wondered if he had any nieces living in Alturas.

"Nothing. And I've been out there twice and looked around." An image of the neighbor, dressed in his bib overalls, came to mind. Maybe he was right about the aliens, but I didn't share this insight with Miss DeLoure. "Look, if anything comes up, I'll let you know. Until then..." I stood and adjusted my gun belt. "I suggest you just run the ad for the reward." Then I left.

Chapter 16

I'm telling you, we have a real situation down here."
Bob Robertson was borderline hysterical.

Waking with almost no muscle stiffness and a lei-surely start to the day updating my evidence board and working on reports had me hopeful. However, any assumptions I'd made about Tuesday being a normal day evaporated quickly. "What kind of situation, Mr. Robertson?" I asked, hesitant to hear the answer.

"A snake. A damn big snake. In fact, it may be the culprit taking my crias."

"Do you know what kind of snake it is?" I rubbed the recently discovered creases between my eyes in an effort to thwart the oncoming headache.

"Haven't seen anything like it in my life."

I didn't understand why he was calling me rather than just killing the thing, but since he had, I was obligated to check it out. "I'll be there shortly," I informed him and then disconnected. Heading south, I decided to stop by the Silver Spur Saloon and see if the resident snake expert might want to tag along.

Parking in front of the Spur, I wasn't surprised to find Pete's maroon '67 Pontiac GTO the only vehicle there. Although he was usually at the bar by midmorning, it didn't open for business until after two. I'd only been there a couple of times during off-hours and found it curiously different — quieter and somehow more inviting. *No wonder he spends so much time here.*

"Howdy Sarah," Pete called as I stepped into the dim interior. "How's my favorite pit crew member?" That familiar smile spread across his face as he moved down the bar toward me.

"Hey." I slid my sunglasses to the top of my head and sat down on the closest barstool. "I'm recovering."

Pete came around and joined me. "Yeah, me too," he said, rubbing his left bicep. "Yesterday I could hardly move. So, what brings you to the Spur on such a fine morning?"

"I was wondering if you'd like to go on an adventure."

"What kind of adventure?"

I filled him in on the missing alpacas and the report of a big snake. "I just thought taking my own snake wrangler would be a good idea."

"No problemo. I'll be happy to go and see what I can do. Just gimme a sec to lock up first." He hopped off his barstool and headed toward the back of the bar. While he secured the place, I returned to my unit and got on the radio to let Cindy know the situation and where I was going.

"Ugh, I hate snakes," Cindy said.

"Yeah, I know," I chuckled. "I'll let you know how it goes."

"No need — really don't care. Just be careful."

"Copy that. 113, 10-26." As I replaced the mic, Pete climbed in. I fired up the Explorer, and we headed south.

Twenty minutes later, we pulled into Bob Robertson's driveway, but no one came rushing over to meet us. In fact, the place seemed unusually quiet. Looking around as we strolled toward the back door, I noticed the LGD had been moved to the front field where the male alpacas were grazing. Just as I raised my hand to knock, Bob came around the corner of the house.

"There's only two of you!" he exclaimed. "You're gonna need more than just the two of you!"

Pete and I exchanged glances. "Mr. Robertson," I began, "we're here to access the situation come up with the next course of action. Do you know Pete here?"

"Yes, yes, of course." They shook hands.

"Can you show me where you last saw the snake?" I asked.

He led us to the gate of the big field, but this time it was empty. "By the pond over yonder is where I came across that snake," he said as he pointed to the right. "But I'm not going back over there."

"Where are the animals that were in this field?" I asked.

"Locked up tight where they'll be safe." He nodded toward the barn. "Now if you'll excuse me, I have some things to take care of." He started toward the outbuilding. "Watch yourselves," he warned just before disappearing inside.

Again Pete and I looked at each other. "Guess some people really don't like snakes," he offered.

"Guess not."

We walked across the field and approached the pond, carefully placing our feet so as not to inadvertently step on anything slithering through the grass.

"Pretty much looks like it did the last two times I was out here," I said as we made our way through the willows on the backside of the pond. "You see anything?"

"Nothing that looks like — hold on, what's that?" Pete said, pointing into the pond.

At first I couldn't see anything amongst all the vegetation until he grabbed a stick and slowly lifted the tip of a tail out of the water. An olive green color, it had splotches of black on it. "Do you know what kind of snake that is?" I asked.

"It's nothing I readily recognize." Stepping down closer to the edge, he used the stick to maneuver the tail closer until he could grab it.

"Careful," I cautioned. "We don't know if it's poisonous or not."

"Only one way to find out," Pete said as he began pulling the tail further out of the pond. "Man, this thing is heavy." He'd exposed about three feet of the snake when I realized something was very wrong.

"Pete, let go and step back," I ordered.

"Why? We still don't know what kind of snake this is." He tugged on the tail again.

Assuming he couldn't see what he had ahold of from his vantage point, I grabbed the collar of his two-tone bowling shirt and gently tugged. "This snake is way too big for you to handle alone."

"What are you talking about?"

"Pete! It's this big around!" I exclaimed, holding my hands up in a circle six inches in diameter. About that time, a huge coil lifted out of the water.

He froze for only an instant, his eyes almost as big as the diameter of the snake. Then he let go of the reptile and quickly backed away from the pond.

"Good call," he said without taking his eyes off the water. "Thanks."

"Come on," I said leading the way back to my unit. "I need to notify the office and see about getting some help to capture that thing." While I talked to Cindy, I sent Pete back to the pond with a roll of crime scene tape and strict directions not to get too close. I'd just finished when an all-too-familiar metallic pink Cadillac came to a screeching stop, quickly reversed, and pulled into the driveway in a cloud of dust.

"Young woman," Marjorie Callaghan called as she exited her vehicle, leaving the driver side door hanging open and the engine running. "I need to speak with you."

With no immediate means of escape, I went to meet her. "Yes Mrs. Callaghan, what can I do for you?"

"Some maniac on a motorcycle practically ran me off the road yesterday. I'd just left Eloise's place and met him on the first curve. He was clear over in my lane!"

"Did you happen to recognize who was driving?"

"No idea who it was, but I want him apprehended and a citation issued!"

"I'll keep an eye out for him, ma'am."

She nodded once and headed back toward her car. "See that you do, young woman." She climbed back in, slammed the door and flipped a U-turn, barely missing the Explorer, before pulling back onto County Road 1 and scattering gravel in her wake.

"Was that Mrs. Callaghan?" Pete asked, coming up beside me.

"Yes, with a complaint about a reckless driver."

"She should know." His crystal-blue eyes twinkled with mischief. "I've seen her drive!" He handed over what was left of the tape. "All taken care of."

"Thanks, you're a good partner. Just don't tell Remy I said so."

A big grin erupted on his face. "Deal!"

"Told you it'd take more than just the two of you," Bob Robertson called as he burst out the backdoor. "You gotta get that thing out of here!"

"I have my dispatcher working on that right now. I'll have her contact you as soon as we find someone who can remove the snake. Until then just stay away from the pond. Come on, Pete."

"What I don't understand," I told Pete a few minutes later as we headed north, "is how that snake got there."

"Yeah, that is a puzzler. In order to keep them calm for transport, most snakes are placed in bags. And a snake that size would have to be transported in some kind of large container."

"Like a wooden crate? A big wooden crate?"

"Yeah, that would work."

It all dropped into place. The snake had escaped from the back of the victim's truck. The smell on the bag was familiar because it was the same reptilian smell from the dozens of lizards I'd caught as a child. "Do you know what mechanical asphyxiation is?" I asked Pete.

"Doesn't that mean being crushed so much you can't breathe?"

Of course! "I know how the snake got there." I quickly explained about finding the truck with the large bag and wooden box in the back, the dead body by the creek that runs just north of the alpaca ranch, the V-shaped wounds on his head and arm, and the cause of death.

"So the guy must have inadvertently let the snake loose, and it killed him and then took up residence in that pond, eating baby alpacas when it got hungry," Pete said.

"That's what I'm thinking." I pulled up to the Spur and shut off the engine. "What I don't know is why he would be transporting such a big snake. Do you think it was his pet?"

"Doubtful. Most people get rid of a snake like that when it no longer fits in its glass cage. Maybe it was stolen."

"I'll have Cindy check into that; see if there's been any reports of a missing giant snake. Thanks again for going with me."

"You bet. Glad to spend time with my favorite deputy." He grinned and winked at me. "Wanna come in and share my sandwich? It's almost lunchtime."

For a split second I actually considered it but wanted to get a jump on my report. "Think I'll pass this time. I need to get home and take care of the pending paperwork. Thanks anyway." Pete climbed out, and I started to put my hand on the gearshift but rolled down my window instead. "Do you think Shellie would watch the bar for a little while tonight?" I called.

He stopped and turned around. "Sure. Why?"

"I'm supposed to meet some of the guys at Lenny's tonight and was wondering if you'd like to tag along. Maybe see what it's like on the other side of the mountain."

"Should be fun. Meet me here, and we'll go over

the pass in the GTO. Don't get to show her off very often."

His enthusiasm made me smile. "I'll be here between 6:00 and 6:30."

By the time I got to Fort Bidwell, I decided to stop by and give Remy an update on my investigations. Past experience taught me my self-appointed partner didn't like hearing about my cases from someone else, especially my sister. Besides, I figured that telling it to someone would help me organize the reports I had to write. I pulled into his driveway just in time to see him walk from the garage toward the garden around back, followed by a miniature mutt, a white goat, and the fawn. *Unbelievable!*

A few minutes later, I was sitting at his kitchen table. He'd insisted on making me a pickle loaf sandwich, complete with lettuce and tomato, while I filled him in on what Pete and I found in the pond.

"What in tarnation is a snake like that doing in Surprise Valley? How did it get there?"

"Must've been in the back of the dead guy's truck. It's the why that I'm still trying to figure out," I said as I watched him make our lunch. "By the way, do you think it's a good idea to let that fawn out of the pen?"

"Don't see why not. Little tike follows me around just like the other two." He set my sandwich in front of me, and my stomach growled a thank you.

"Well, the BLM is supposed to be getting back to me in the next day or two," I reminded him. "Someone will be coming by to pick it up and take it to a rehabilitation place."

"Then what?" Remy joined me with his own sandwich.

"When the fawn is old enough, they release it back into the wild."

"Well hells bells, I can do that. Ain't no need for that little fella to be taken anywheres else."

"But Remy, it's not legal for you to keep him. Besides, they already know about it."

He glared at me. "Just don't seem right."

We finished our lunch in silence. I thanked him for my sandwich and then proceeded on to my place. After completing my reports on the dead body and missing crias, I called Cindy. "Any luck finding someone to come get that snake?"

"Not yet. The closest snake mover is in San Jose. How big did you say that snake was anyway?"

"I'm not sure — at least ten feet if not bigger."

"Ten feet or bigger?" she exclaimed.

"That's why we need to get it removed as soon as possible."

"Why not just kill it?"

"Can't get close enough to find the head as long as it's hiding under the vegetation in that pond. Besides, it may have been stolen. I want you to check around for any snakes over ten feet in length that have been reported missing within a 500-mile radius of Surprise Valley."

"Will do. By the way, are you coming to Lenny's tonight?"

"Yeah, I think so."

"Great. Archie and I are going, so we can hang out together."

"Okay, sounds good." I hung up, anxious to find out more about this teacher from New Zealand.

Chapter 17

It was just a few minutes past seven when Pete and I pulled up in front of Lenny's Bar and Grill. I recognized the majority of the vehicles parked there, including Cindy's Chevy Impala. *Should be an interesting evening, to say the least.*

As we pushed through the doors, I spotted Scott seated at the long table in the back along with Josh Green from the lab and several other deputies. A quick scan revealed Cindy and her new friend at a high table near one of the windows.

"Why don't you grab us a couple of beers and I'll go see how things are going," I suggested.

"No problemo," Pete replied. "I'll be there in a minute." He stepped over to the bar and was instantly greeted.

"Pete!"

"Lenny, how's it going?"

The two men reached across the bar, grasping right hands with their thumbs up, and gave each other a man hug like two long lost friends. I likened it to the waves of acceptance shared by motorcycle riders and RV drivers alike. Leaving the bartenders to bond, I continued on to the large group of off-duty law enforcement officers.

"Howdy Sarah, glad you could make it."

"Hi Scott. Looks like the party is in full swing." Everyone had at least one empty in front of him, some had two.

Scott's crooked smile appeared. "Some of us got kind of a head start."

"And who's the DD?" I asked.

Josh raised his hand. "That would be me. I even borrowed my mom's minivan."

"Let's hear it for the minivan." Scott raised his beer in the air.

"To the minivan," the others chimed in, doing the same.

"Aw, come on you guys. Cut it out." Josh slouched in his seat.

"I hope you're charging these bozos for a ride," I said.

"You bet. Five bucks a head — ten if they puke."

"Better make it twenty." I winked at him; he smiled and nodded.

"Here you go." Pete handed me a Corona.

"Thanks."

He looked around the table. "Where's Sheriff... Sheriff... what's his name?"

"Chet Atkins," I replied, and then we all looked at Scott.

"What?" he asked as soon as he realized we were all staring at him.

"So where is he, Scott? Giving a concert somewhere?" offered one of the deputies sitting at the other end of the table. The rest of them laughed.

"Or having his guitar restrung?" another one added. More laughter.

"Knock it off!" Scott exclaimed. "That's not funny!"

Pete leaned over and whispered, "I don't get it."

"Scott used to think making fun of the Sheriff's name was the most hilarious thing ever, until the Sheriff caught him and made him work a double shift, which included hauling a dead body to Redding. Guess he's learned his lesson." I turned back to the table. "No Sandusky either?"

"We kept this thing hush-hush," Scott said. There were nods around the table. "Didn't need Dirk the Jerk here being a buzzkill." I seriously doubted Sandusky didn't know about the gathering. My own experience with the man had taught me that very little gets by the Undersheriff.

"Go ahead and join us," Josh said. "There's room and I could use the cash!"

There were only two empty seats, one on each end. Glancing over my shoulder, I noticed Cindy waving at us. "Thanks, we will in a little while, but first I guess we better go say hi." Looping my arm through Pete's, I led the way back to the front of the place where the newly formed couple was waiting.

"About time the two of you joined us," Cindy said as we each climbed onto a stool. "Archie, this is Pete. He owns the Silver Spur Saloon — the place we went to last Saturday. Pete this is Archie."

"Howdy." Pete extended his right hand.

"G'day mate," Archie replied, doing the same and exposing a glimpse of some kind of tattoo beneath the short sleeve of his yellow plaid shirt.

"And you remember Sarah?" Cindy continued.

He brushed the brim of his ball cap with two fingers. "Miss."

An awkward silence settled over us as we sipped

our beers. Finally Pete spoke up. "So, what brings you to Alturas?"

"Just passing through mostly but ran low on petrol and cash," Archie said, scratching his chin through his neatly trimmed beard. "But I've decided to stay around for a wee bit." He smiled at Cindy, and she smiled back at him.

Pete chuckled. "Me too — about ten years ago. The area seems to grow on you after a while. Where are you from originally?"

"Archie's from New Zealand, right?" I said before he had a chance to answer.

"That's right." He adjusted his cap, pulling it slightly lower over his dark eyes and revealing close-cropped, bleached blond hair.

"And he rides motorcycles too." I added.

"Really?" Pete placed both elbows on the table and leaned in. "Street or dirt?"

"Uh, street mostly. You?"

"I enjoy both, but dirt is my favorite; the wide open spaces, relying on your own riding skill. In fact, I've been considering signing up for the Great Australian Ride; over seven thousand kilometers in twenty days, across two deserts." He picked up his beer and took a long draw. "Man, talk about a challenge."

"I hear you. Thought about that myself when I was younger but decided to keep my wheels on the pavement."

Pete frowned for just a second. "Yeah."

"Cindy tells me you were teaching back east. Whereabouts?" I asked, hoping to steer the conversation in a different direction.

Archie turned slightly to the right and, without

making eye contact with me, replied, "Upstate New York mostly."

"Upstate New York. Really? And when does your work visa run out?" Suddenly, I received a sharp kick to my shin.

Cindy picked up her Budweiser and drained it. "Would you mind getting me another, Archie dear?" After he'd left the table, she turned on me. "Will you please stop giving him the third degree? You're making him uncomfortable."

"I didn't mean to — just making conversation." I glanced at Pete who seemed fascinated with a gouge in the tabletop. "Look Cindy..." I leaned closer to her. "There's something going on with this guy," I said, watching him weave around the tables as he made his way to the U-shaped bar. "Something is just not right."

She stared at me for a second or two. "Knock it off, okay? You don't need to protect me; I can take care of myself. It's not like I'm going to run off with the guy, and I seriously doubt he's a serial killer." She grabbed her purse. "Now, if you will excuse us, we are going to celebrate our one week anniversary privately." She hopped off the stool and went over to where Archie was awaiting his turn at the bar. After a brief exchange, the two of them left.

"That went well," Pete said, grinning at me.

I playfully slapped at his arm. "Oh shut up. I'm really concerned for her. She's been looking for a guy for so long I'm afraid she isn't seeing this one for what he truly is."

"He seems okay to me. But..."

"But what?"

"Well, remember when I mentioned the Great Australian Ride?"

"Yeah."

"I just thought his comment was strange. The ride has only been in existence for a couple of years." He finished off his beer. "Maybe he was thinking of some other race."

"Maybe." I swirled my beer in the bottle before downing it.

Pete slid off his stool. "That tattoo of his was some coincidence, though."

"I didn't get a good look at it. What was it?"

"Not sure, but I think it was the tail of a snake."

"A snake?"

"Yeah. Crazy, huh?" He headed toward the bathrooms located in the back.

"Yeah, crazy." Maybe I was making more of the whole situation than was really there. And if anyone could take care of herself, it was Cindy.

Loud raucous laughter erupted from the table of Sheriff's Office staff, and I could see Scott telling some bullshit story of his, complete with wild arm gestures. I abandoned the tall table and headed over, stopping by the bar long enough to grab two more Coronas. Pete spotted me as he walked by, and together we joined the party.

Three games of pool, two orders of onion rings, and a Reuben sandwich split between us later, we helped Josh load his passengers into the minivan and bade them good-bye. Then we climbed into Pete's GTO and headed over the pass. My last recollection was snuggling up next to him as the muscle car flew up the mountain.

Chapter 18

It is going to kill him. Absolutely kill him. I had no idea how I was going to tell Remy the biologist from the BLM had called and was on her way to pick up the fawn. Not really wanting to tell him in person, I dialed his number instead.

"It's Sarah," I began when he answered. "The biologist from the BLM just called and she's..." There was a click on the line and then nothing. "Remy? Are you still there?" Silence. *Damn!*

I tossed my cell phone into the passenger seat, flipped a U-turn, and headed for Fort Bidwell. Based in Cedarville, I knew the biologist had a few minutes headstart. I just hoped I got there before Remy did something he'd regret.

Pulling into his driveway a while later, I was not surprised to see him standing, Millie and Bubbles at his feet, spraddle-legged with his arms folded across his chest. The biologist was facing him and, judging by her gestures, trying to convince him to surrender the fawn. However, when I climbed out of my patrol unit, I noticed something more disturbing. The gate to the pen was open, and the pen was empty.

"Hi," I said as I approached. "I'm Sarah Murdock."

"Bonnie Patterson," the biologist replied. "Pleased

to meet you. I was just explaining to Mr. Hamilton here what happens to orphaned fawns that are rescued. Unfortunately, he tells me the fawn is no longer here."

"No longer here? But I saw it yesterday, Remy. What happened to it?"

He motioned toward the pen. "Don't rightly know. Must not have latched the gate tight last night, and the little tike got out. Haven't seen hide nor hair of him today."

"He might be bedded down close by," Bonnie suggested. "Mind if we look around?"

"Look around all you want." Remy swept his arm in a large arc. "I got better things to do than look for a damn deer. Come on you two," he said to his small companions. "Let's get busy on our chores."

"I'll head this way," Bonnie said, pointing to the left, "if you want to circle around the other way and we'll meet on the far side. Check in and under every bush within twenty feet of the clearing."

For the next hour, we diligently searched for the fawn. Several times during the search, I looked over at Remy only to find him chopping away at weeds and mopping his sweaty brow occasionally with the blue and white handkerchief he keeps in his back pocket. Finally, the biologist and I met on the far side of the clearing surrounding Remy's house, but neither one of us had seen any sign of the small deer.

"I'm sorry," I said. "Looks like I got you up here on a wild goose chase."

"Don't you mean a wild fawn chase?" She smiled. "It's okay. It may show up again. If it does, just give me a call." Then she walked back to her rig and drove off.

I strolled over to where Remy was working and stood, my right hand resting on the butt of my Sig 9mm and the thumb of my left hand hooked into my gun belt. "So what'd you do with it?"

He straightened up and leaned the hoe against the fence surrounding the garden. "Don't know what you're talking about." He mopped his head again.

"You told me yourself, that fawn follows you everywhere. There's no way it wandered off."

He studied his boots and shook his head.

"Remy," I said, placing my hand on his shoulder, "partners don't keep secrets from each other."

His head jerked up, and he glared at me for only a second before his gaze softened. "Doggone it! Why'd you have to go and play the partner card?" He snatched his black felt hat off a nearby fence post and started toward the front of his double-wide. I followed him past the wood shed and along the driveway to the pump house where he jammed his hat on his head before pulling a wad of keys from his pocket and opening the padlock, which hung from the hasp on the door. Stepping inside, I wasn't surprised to see the missing fawn curled up on the quilt I'd previously seen in Remy's house.

"Couldn't bear thinking of Buck being all alone again."

"Buck?"

Remy gave me a sheepish grin and shrugged. "Had to call him something besides Fawn." *Good grief!* He made a clicking sound with his tongue, and the little deer scrambled to his feet and joined the other two animals that had followed us. After performing the typical nose-to-nose ritual, the trio frolicked out of sight.

"Remy, you can't..." His expression made me stop. I'd played the partner card; therefore, I must honor the partner code. "Fine," I said, holding my arms up in surrender.

His short white beard and trimmed mustache seemed to grow as a huge grin blossomed on his face. "You'll see. It'll be just fine. That little fella will grow up and be off on his own before you know it."

I shook my head. "As far as I'm concerned, it ran off. If asked, I haven't seen it. But be forewarned, that biologist may just stop by one day to see if it turned up. If she does, you're on your own."

"Understood." He saluted against the wide brim of his hat. "Besides," he said, securing the pump house door, "I think Bubba's taken a shine to that fawn."

"Bubba? You mean Bubbles?"

"Course I do. Ain't right to call him by some sissy name."

Somehow, I didn't think my sister would agree, but I wasn't going there. Not now. "Look Remy, I have to get back to work. I'll see you later."

"Alrighty then." He started off in the same directions as the animals. Just as I reached my patrol unit, he stopped and turned around. "How 'bout I fix us dinner, seeing as how you ain't been over for a spell."

"You fixed me lunch just yesterday."

"Oh hell, that don't count. I'll fry us up some pork chops and make mashed taters and gravy."

I laughed. "Sounds good, Remy. I'll be looking forward to it." I'd just left Fort Bidwell when I got an incoming call on my cell phone. Inaccessible in my front left pocket, I pulled to the side of the road before digging it out. I recognized the number and connected. "Murdock."

"It *was* stolen!"

"Okayyy. What was stolen?"

"That damn snake." Cindy continued in her official dispatcher's voice. "Approximately two weeks ago, the Las Vegas Zoo discovered its twenty-foot green anaconda had been taken. They warned that the snake is extremely dangerous and all contact should be avoided. They will be sending a catch team as soon as possible, but it may be as late as Monday before they can get here."

"Got it. I'll let Bob Robertson know. Thanks, Cindy." I hung up and immediately dialed the alpaca rancher and gave him the news. His tone and choice of words clearly indicated he was not pleased having to wait so long to get rid of the snake, but I explained there was nothing more I could do. At least for now.

Before pulling back onto County Road 1 and continuing my patrol, I made one more phone call. "Miss DeLoure," I requested when a young woman answered.

"One moment please," she replied, attempting to suppress a giggle. I assumed it was one of the women I'd spoken to at the front desk of the *Alturas Gazette's* office. When Lulu answered, I quickly explained about the discovery of the snake believed responsible for the missing crias and the catch team coming to remove it. "Perhaps covering the story might be the break you're looking for," I suggested.

"Oh, thank you so much for the heads up," she said. "Maybe I should go out and take some preliminary pictures."

"I don't think that would be a good idea, you see..."

"And I could interview the rancher." Her

enthusiasm was building. "You know, get a feel for the story."

"Unless your paper is into printing four letter words, I don't think you'd get much out of Mr. Robertson."

"Then I'll just stick to taking a few photographs."

"Under no circumstances are you to go out there until I notify you the catch team is on its way. It's way too dangerous."

"Fine!" Then she mumbled something I couldn't quite make out and hung up.

A few more days. A few more days for life to get back to normal. The investigation into the missing alpacas had been resolved, although not how Mr. Robertson would have preferred. The dead body had been identified as well as the cause of death. The issue of the orphaned fawn had been dealt with, at least for the time being. The giant cria-eating snake would be gone soon and its threat removed.

However, not every case had been closed. I still had no leads on Pete's stolen motorcycle, and I hadn't received a single call regarding the goat I'd found — not that Remy would agree to give it up now anyway. And the same went for Bubbles. I was surprised the dumb dog got to come home with me.

Then there was Cindy's new boyfriend. Despite my concerns, she'd basically told me to back off and mind my own business. As much as I hated to do it, I really had no choice or risk losing her as a friend. All I could do was hope Archie moved on soon. Focusing on dinner with Remy, I managed to survive the rest of my patrol.

Chapter 19

"That looks delicious," I said as Remy placed a platter of crispy pork chops on the table. A giant pile of fluffy, white mashed potatoes sat next to it. While I grabbed us a couple of Miller beers out of the fridge, he added a big bowl of steaming hot green beans seasoned with what looked like at least a pound of bacon.

"This here's the end of last summer's crop. Enjoy, because it'll be a couple of months before there's any new crop to pick." He pulled out a chair and motioned for me to do the same. "Now, set yourself down for a spell." Without hesitation, I did as I was told.

Before heading to Remy's after my shift was done, I'd driven home and exchanged my uniform for a baggy pair of jeans and an oversized T-shirt. Then I spent a few minutes scratching the small, white star in the middle of Raven's flat forehead while he munched on his flake of hay. "This weekend we'll play," I promised him. Ready for a relaxing evening, I'd walked the short distance to Remy's.

He returned to the stove and retrieved a crock from the oven. "Here's the gravy for the taters," he said, placing it in front of me.

My mouth watered as I filled my plate with the comfort food; a mound of mashed potatoes and a thick pork chop smothered in gravy with a generous helping of bacon green beans. I popped the top to my beer, anticipating that first sip — and my cell phone rang. I considered ignoring it until...

"Ain't you gonna answer that?" Remy asked. "Might be something urgent?"

"That's what I'm afraid of." I put down my beer and dug my phone out of my pocket. Seeing an unfamiliar number, again I was tempted to ignore the call but thought better of it. I flipped it open and hit the green button. "Hello."

"Sarah?" I didn't recognize the voice. "This is Cindy, and I'm in terrible trouble." Her voice was weak and shaky."Cindy, what's wrong? Where are you?" For a split second, I wondered why she wasn't calling me on her cell phone; she never went anywhere without it.

"Oh help me! It's..." I jumped as a loud slapping sound cut her off.

"Cindy! Where are you?" I yelled. Barely audible, a voice in the background was too muffled to make out what was being said. Finally, Cindy came back on the line.

"Sarah, he'll let me go if you come get me, but only you."

"Who will let you go? Archie?" *I knew that guy was bad news.*

"I can't tell you. And you have to come alone. Nobody else or he'll — he'll..." Another pause. "He'll kill me," she whispered.

Oh shit! "Okay relax, I'm coming. Where are you?"

"The old abandoned church in Eagleville. Around

back you'll see the entrance into the..." She sobbed a couple of times. "I'm in the basement."

"Hang on, Cindy! I'll be there as soon as I can." I snapped the phone shut and stuffed it back into my pocket. "Remy, I'm sorry but I have to go." Glancing at him, I almost laughed.

His eyes were as huge as the pork chops, and his hand had stopped mid-serve, gravy dripping from the ladle onto the red and white checkered table-cloth. "What'd ya mean you have to go?" He looked at the mess he was making and plopped the ladle back into the crock of gravy. "You can't be serious about going there alone."

"I take it you heard both sides of that conversation."

"Every word. Give me a quick second," he jerked his chin toward his Marlin .45-70 rifle hanging next to the front door, "and me and ol' Bessie will back you up."

The man does have a knack for naming things.
"No Remy, it's too dangerous." I pushed back from the table and started for the door. Bubbles, who was curled up with Millie in their usual spot next to Remy's chair, raised his head as I went by. "You stay here. Don't need you getting in my way." I rushed out and hustled to the end of the driveway. Then I broke into a run, wondering how a seemingly short distance could suddenly take forever to cover. When I finally reached my place, I was out of breath and anxious to get on the road but knew I needed to do a few things before leaving.

Yanking off my shirt, I located my body armor under the pile of clothes I'd left on the floor of my bedroom and strapped it on. I covered it with a dark blue T-shirt and a long-sleeved shirt, which I left unbuttoned. I reached for the Smith and Wesson .38 Special in my bedside stand but decided carrying it in my shoulder holster was too conspicuous. Instead, I retrieved the Nike shoebox from the top shelf of my closet and strapped on the ankle holster for my Kel-Tec .380 pocket pistol. After making sure the six-round clip was fully loaded, I slammed it into place and holstered the weapon.

As I grabbed my keys and started out the door, Remy's words nagged at me. *Am I really going to handle this alone?* Not wanting to be foolish, I picked up the landline and dialed the office.

"Modoc County Sheriff's Office."

"Sandusky?"

"Speaking."

"This is Sarah. Why are you answering the phone?"

"Well, if you must know, Murdock, Fielding called in sick again, and I couldn't get a hold of Cindy. With the Sheriff and Jenkins gone, we're shorthanded, so I'm covering dispatch. Now, was there something you needed, or is this just a social call?"

"I know why you couldn't reach Cindy."

"Well bully for you. Is that why you called?"

I tried a different approach. "Look Dirk..."

"Undersheriff Sandusky to you, Murdock. Now what the hell do you want?"

"Cindy's in trouble and..."

"And just how do you know Cindy's in trouble?"

"Sandusky, will you shut up and listen? I need your help! I think she's being held in an abandoned church in Eagleville, and if I don't get there soon, he's going to kill her?"

"Who's gonna kill her?"

"She couldn't tell me, but I'm pretty sure it's that guy she's been seeing. I need you to go by her place and make sure she's not there. She lives..."

Sandusky interrupted. "I know where she lives."

"Then I need you to meet me in Cedarville, and we can go on to Eagleville from there. The only thing is, you need to be in an unmarked car because I'm supposed to go there alone."

There was a long pause before he answered. "Get one thing straight, Murdock. I'm doing this for Cindy, not you."

"Fine, whatever. But we have to move now. Call when you get to Cindy's and let me know what you find." I gave him my cell number and disconnected.

Minutes ticked by and no word. *Damn it, Sandusky!* Afraid to wait any longer, I snatched my keys off the desk, climbed into the Dooley and fired it up. I was a few miles south of Fort Bidwell when my phone finally went off.

"Well?"

"She's gone all right and so is her car. I'm guessing you may be right. There's a red Harley parked here."

"Yeah, that's gotta be Archie's"

"Funny thing, though..." It sounded like he was walking around. "Looks like it's recently been painted and not too well. There's red paint on the spokes and splatters on the seat."

"Scrape off some paint and tell me what color it used to be."

There was a rustling sound as he jostled his phone. "Black."

"Is there some kind of mark or blemish on the seat?"

"Yeah, on the left side."

Son-of-a-bitch! Pete's bike! "Okay, I'm heading for Eagleville now. The church should be on Main Street, and I'm supposed to enter through the basement around back."

"Got it. I'll be there shortly. Try not to get yourself killed in the meantime," he jeered and hung up.

"Asshole," I muttered, snapping my phone shut and slipping it into the cupholder of the center console.

It was dusk when I drove through Cedarville and completely dark by the time I parked in front of the boarded up building in Eagleville. Putting my phone on silent, I shoved it deep into my pocket, grabbed my miniature MagLite out of the glove compartment, and headed toward the back of the building. Cindy's Impala was parked near the stairs going into the basement. Shining the light down the stairwell, I saw the door was slightly ajar. Whether or not to retrieve my concealed weapon crossed my mind, but I decided to leave it where it was until I needed it.

Cautiously, I moved down the stairs and pulled the door open just enough to peer inside. A long narrow hallway led deep into the building with several doors leading off from it. Slowly and silently, I searched each one in turn, expecting each time to find Cindy crumpled in some corner, but all I found was cobwebs, dust and an occasional broken piece of furniture. Finally, I reached the door at the end of the hallway and pushed it open.

The room seemed much larger than the others, but it was hard to tell as it was pitch black — except, that is, where Cindy was. Bathed in the faint light of a battery-operated lantern sitting on the floor behind her, she sat in a dilapidated chair, her wrists and ankles secured to it with duct tape. Her curly brown hair was matted and hung in her face. When I whispered her name, her head jerked up, revealing a strip of the tape across her mouth and a look of terror in her eyes.

"Are you okay?" I tucked my flashlight into my front pocket and crept toward her, my eyes attempting to penetrate the sea of darkness that surrounded us. As I got closer, I could see her eyes were red and puffy, and a crimson, hand-shaped welt covered her left cheek.

"Do you know where he is?" I asked, reaching out to take hold of the tape on her face. She squeezed her eyes shut and shook her head. "This might hurt a bit." I managed to get hold of a corner of it and slowly pulled, lifting the skin of her face with it until it finally released its sticky grip.

"Hurry Sarah!" Cindy begged as I picked at the duct tape binding her right wrist to the arm of the chair. "I don't know where he went or when he'll be back!"

Tugging and pulling at the tape, I cursed myself for not bringing my Swiss Army Knife. I almost had her free when the double clack of an automatic handgun's slide being pulled back and released shattered the silence.

"Omigod, he's in here!" Cindy wailed.

A malevolent chuckle came from the deep darkness directly behind her. Again I toyed with the idea of pulling my pocket pistol out of its hiding place but knew there wasn't enough time for it to be effective. *Where the hell is Sandusky?*

"Is that you, Archie?" I called, trying to be as

nonchalant as my racing heart would allow. Cindy began vigorously shaking her head. "Not Archie?" I whispered to her. She nodded, shook her head again, and then rolled her eyes.

"For a while I pretended to be Archie," came the reply in that familiar down-under accent. "But not anymore!" The accent was gone and that pang of familiarity hit me again. The scuffling of boots and a faint glow of white emerged from the darkness and came closer until he stepped into the dim glow. Camouflage pants over military style boots and topped with a wife beater, the man stood there, aiming the gun at my torso and grinning with a satisfaction that made my stomach clench. His snake tattoo was clearly visible, starting just above the elbow and winding itself up his right arm and over his shoulder, its head disappearing under the white undershirt.

"What do you want?" I asked, trying to keep the tremor out of my voice.

"You still don't know, do you?" Keeping the gun trained on me, he removed his ball cap and tossed it into the darkness. "Don't care for the hair," he said, skimming his head with his free hand, "but I think I'm going to keep the beard."

Looking at Cindy, I frowned and slowly shook my head.

"What's the matter, Murdock? Your woman's intuition don't work anymore?"

Then I knew; the realization hitting me so hard I took a step back. "Hensley!"

Chapter 20

W ho's Hensley?" Cindy asked, her gaze darting from me to the man with the gun and back again.

Without taking my eyes off him, I held up my hand. "Long story — tell you later. So now what, Richard?"

"We get reacquainted and then it's payback time for fucking up my life!" his lip curling into a snarl as he spoke.

"What about Cindy?" I asked as I nodded my head once in her direction.

"Oh, I got something real nice planned for her." He switched the gun to his left hand and pulled a Buck knife from its sheath on his belt.

"Sarah!" Cindy wailed again, pulling against her restraints.

"Here," he said, flipping the knife so he was holding the tip. "Cut her loose but don't try anything heroic, or I'll pop you right here."

I took the knife and carefully slid the blade under Cindy's right wrist and along the arm of the chair. "Hold real still so I don't cut you," I warned.

"Okay," she whispered, nodding slightly. As I

freed her legs, she rubbed her wrists as well as the welt on her cheek.

"Your turn," Hensley said to me as soon as she was free. "But first, hand me back the knife."

For a split second, I considered lunging at him. Had I been alone, I might have but waiting for Sandusky to make his move would certainly shift the odds in our favor. I handed over the knife, which he slid back into its sheath. Then he pulled out a bundle of cable ties and handed them to Cindy. "Tie her hands behind her back, and then I'll do you." She hesitated, her eyes locked on mine.

"It's okay, do as he says," I urged, turning around and holding out my hands. She fumbled, dropping some of them before she managed to secure two of them, holding my wrists together. Right away I realized she hadn't completely tightened them. *Atta girl, Cindy!*

"Pick those up and give them to me," Hensley ordered, pointing to the cable ties at her feet. As soon as Cindy handed them over, he spun her around and quickly secured her hands behind her back. "Now, we're ready to go." He grabbed the lantern and waved the gun twice, indicating we were to move toward the door, which was barely visible outside the ring of light.

"Hold on," he said just as we reached it. "Get on your knees, Love, while I check your work." The accent was back, but this time Cindy wasn't impressed, scowling at him as she knelt down. Stepping closer to me, he placed the portable light on the floor and checked the narrow strips of plastic encircling my wrists. "Why Cindy, I'm disappointed. These are way too loose to be effective." He took hold of the tail end of each one and gave it a good yank, pinching the skin on the inside of my wrists. "There, much better. Now let's get moving." Keeping the gun pointed at me, he took hold of Cindy's left elbow and helped her to her feet. Then he retrieved the lantern and swung it toward the door. "After you."

By the time we reached the end of the hallway, my hands began to throb, and I knew it wouldn't be long until they were completely numb. The window of opportunity for me to do anything was shrinking fast.

Hensley clicked off the light and placed the handle in Cindy's hands. "Drop it and I'll have to punish you again." As she let out a weak gasp, I thought of the welt he'd already put on her face. "And if you have any thoughts of trying anything stupid," he said to me, "my gun is aimed at your friend's ribs, and I won't hesitate to pull the trigger. Now go!"

I had no other choice but to do as he said and wait for Sandusky. As I reached the top of the stairs, I looked around for anyone who might see us, but there were no signs of life in the darkness.

"That's far enough," Hensley said when we reached the back of Cindy's car. He pulled out her keys and opened the trunk. "This is where you ride, Murdock."

It suddenly became harder to breathe as the panic set in. *Now, Sandusky!* "In there?" I gasped. "You want me to ride in there? There's practically no room." It was true. Most of the space was taken up by two bag chairs — minus their bags — a handyman jack, a box of tire chains, an army surplus blanket, and a first-aid kit.

"Sorry Sarah," Cindy whimpered.

"Quit complaining and get in there. Now!" Hensley grabbed my shirt with his free hand and shoved me toward the trunk. Caught off balance, I tumbled backward and fell in. "Good job," he chuckled. "Now don't go away, I'll be right back." He took hold of Cindy's arm and led her toward the front of her vehicle.

Using my legs, I tried to get into a more comfortable position. Landing on my side, the metal poles of the chairs were digging into my hip and shoulder. After thrashing around a couple of times, I managed to roll over on my back with my feet and legs in better position for a surprise attack. All of a sudden, Cindy screamed, and it sounded like somebody hit the ground.

"Cindy, are you all right?" I called as I felt adrenaline surge through my body. "Hensley, don't you hurt her, you bastard!" I threw my legs over the edge of the trunk and propelled myself out, almost falling flat on my face.

"Relax Murdock, everything's under control." It was Sandusky and he was standing next to Cindy's car, holding her as she sobbed quietly against his chest. Hensley was sprawled on the ground behind him, apparently out cold.

"What took you so long?" I said, walking toward him.

"It's all in the timing. I was just waiting for the best time to take him by surprise with the least amount of resistance. And as you can see," he gestured toward Hensley's motionless body, "my plan worked perfectly."

"Cut me loose would you?" I said, turning around. "My hands are killing me."

Cindy sniffled and pushed back from Sandusky.

"Dirk, there's a pair of scissors in the first-aid kit that should work just fine to get these things off our wrists." She led the way back to the open trunk. "It's there," she said, gesturing with her shoulder, "over to the right."

Sandusky fished out the small white box and popped it open. At first, I didn't think the scissors were going to be strong enough, but he kept at it until finally Cindy's cable ties yielded.

"Now cut Sarah loose," she instructed, flexing her fingers.

With no regard to my discomfort, he dispatched one of the ties and handed me the scissors. "Here, you can handle the other one." Then he grabbed the blanket and proceeded to wrap it around Cindy.

Under the glow of the trunk light, my fingers resembled purple sausages, which made it extremely difficult to manipulate the scissors. I'd just cut through the strip of plastic when squealing tires announced the approach of a vehicle traveling at an excessive speed. *Does Hensley have an accomplice?* I looked up just in time to see Remy's Toyota Land Cruiser whip around the corner and skid to a stop a few feet from Cindy's car. He jumped out, his rifle in hand. "You better let go of that gal and stand back," he said, raising Bessie to take aim.

"Hold up, Remy!" I said, raising my hands and stepping in front of him. "He's with me." Just then Pete came around the back of Remy's rig, packing his Louisville Slugger from the bar. "What are you doing here?" I asked.

"Remy swung by the Spur on his way here and filled me in on the situation. I agreed you might need back up, so we got here as soon as we could.

Are you okay?" He wrapped his arm around me, his familiar scent calming and reassuring me. "What's going on?" The concern in his eyes surprised me.

"Turns out Cindy's new boyfriend was only using her to get to me."

"What on earth would a school teacher from New Zealand want with you?" he asked.

"That's just it. He's not who he claims to be, but I didn't figure that out until tonight." I shook my head. "Let's just say we have a history, and he was here to settle an old score."

"So where is this nemesis of yours?" Pete leaned to one side in order to peer around me.

"Lying right over —" But he wasn't. The spot where he'd collapsed was empty.

"What the hell!" Sandusky said, leaving Cindy's side and walking around her car.

My stomach twisted into a knot and, for a second, I thought I was going to throw up. "He must've used the commotion of Remy's arrival to escape." I pulled my flashlight out of my pocket and began searching.

"What in tarnation are you looking for?" Remy asked, trailing behind me.

"His gun."

"Not a problem, Murdock," Sandusky said, pulling the small black automatic handgun from the back of his waistband. "I secured that the second he hit the ground."

"What about his knife?" Cindy asked, pulling the blanket tighter around her shoulders.

"Uh, knife? Didn't see one."

"It was in a sheath on his belt," I said, shining

162

the beam from my flashlight into the surrounding darkness.

"He must've landed on it when I clobbered him."

"Oh!" Cindy exclaimed, as if she'd been jabbed in the ribs. "He's got my keys."

"Oh great. Just what we need — a fugitive with access to a vehicle." Sandusky moved to the other side of Cindy's car, yanked open the driver side door, and released the hood latch.

"Dirk, what are you doing?" Cindy asked.

"Can't leave him a means of escape, so I'm gonna jerk out the battery."

"Hang on a second." I stuffed my flashlight back into my pocket and pulled down the open trunk lid. There, hanging from the lock, were Cindy's keys. Sandusky glared at me.

"Thank goodness," she said, pulling them out and slamming the lid down. "I'd like to go home now."

"I'm not sure that's such a good idea." Sandusky relatched the hood and returned to Cindy's side. "What if this Archie..."

"Hensley," I corrected. "His name is Richard Hensley. He's wanted by the FBI, and he's extremely dangerous."

"My point exactly! Look Cindy," his voice softened as he spoke to her, "he knows where you live and as long as he's on the loose, you're not safe there."

"Well, I suppose I could stay with one of my relatives."

Sandusky shook his head. "No good. That will be the first place he looks. I think you should come home with me, so I can protect you."

This is Dirk the Jerk?

"Well..." She glanced my way. "If you think it's best."

"I do, and I'll drive you home." Sandusky gently took her keys and escorted her to the passenger seat. As he walked back around to the driver's side, he tossed his own keys to me. "The unmarked unit is around front. Make sure you radio in the APB for that guy. We need to apprehend him as soon as possible." Before I could protest, he slid in behind the wheel, started the engine, and drove off.

"Damn it!" I exclaimed, turning to Remy and Pete. "How am I supposed to drive the unmarked unit and my own rig."

"I'd be happy to follow you in the Dooley, and then we can ride back from Alturas together."

Why didn't I think of that? Obviously, my encounter with Hensley had affected me more than I thought. "That's a good idea," I said, moving toward the Land Cruiser. "Remy, will you drive us to the front of the church?" I asked, scanning the area for Hensley.

"You bet, Partner. Pile in."

Pete winked at me as he held the passenger side door open. I smiled back before clambering over the seat and diving into the back.

"You want me and Bessie to stand guard whilst you and Pete get on your way?" Remy offered as we climbed out.

"No, we'll be fine. In fact, I want you to get going right now." I swung the door shut and continued speaking through the open window. "And don't stop for anyone. I don't care if they're standing in the middle of the road. Run over them if you have to but don't stop." I turned to Pete. "That goes for you too!"

"Understood," he and Remy said in unison, which generated a nervous laugh from each of us.

"On your way home, you stop by and we'll have our supper. I got it all tucked away in the oven." He pointed at Pete. "And bring him along. There's plenty to go around."

"Okay, Remy. Will do. Now get going." As he drove off, I reached down and freed my concealed weapon from its holster. Then I again retrieved my flashlight and knelt down next to my Dooley.

"What are you doing?" Pete asked, joining me on the ground.

"Making sure we don't have any unwanted passengers. You and Slugger keep an eye out," I said, sweeping the beam of light along the undercarriage. "Don't need Hensley getting the jump on us!"

"No problemo!" And he was gone.

After checking my truck, I lay down next to the unmarked Crown Vic and checked under it. Satisfied we were alone, I pulled out my set of keys and tossed them to Pete. "Let's get out of here. Pull into the parking lot on the west side of the Sheriff's Office."

"Yessir, Deputy." He flashed me that huge grin of his, smartly saluted, and climbed into my Ford. As soon as he had it started, I fired up the unmarked unit and led the way back to Alturas.

Chapter 21

As I headed north on County Road 1, I could feel the tension building across my shoulders and up into my neck. After requesting the APB on him, I expected to see Hensley jump out in front of my vehicle in an attempt to flag me down. *How did I not recognize him?* Sue had warned me that he might be looking for me, but I hadn't taken her seriously. Cresting Cedar Pass, I finally began to relax when I realized he couldn't have possibly covered that much territory on foot.

By the time I'd parked the car and turned in the keys, the stress of the evening had taken its toll. I could barely keep my eyes open and didn't really care that Pete was still in the driver's seat of my Ford. I pulled myself up into the cab, reclined the seat and closed my eyes. He'd just started to pull out onto Highway 299 when I suddenly remembered. "Wait!"

He stomped on the clutch and brake simultaneously, causing the Dooley to rock. "What!"

"I know where your Harley is!"

"Oh, you know where my — what'd you say?"

"Your bike. I know where it is. Head down Main, toward the park."

Without another word, Pete accelerated across all four lanes of the highway, ignoring the turn lane and any oncoming traffic. Moments later, he turned onto Water Street and drove along the north edge of the park.

"Over there," I said pointing to the left. "It's the house on the corner."

"You sure it's here?" he asked as we glided to a stop in front of the gate.

"Probably around the side, in the driveway."

Pete eased along the curb, turned left and crept along the fence until the headlights reflected off the chrome of a motorcycle. "You sure that's mine?" he asked, shutting down the engine but leaving the headlights on.

"Yeah, pretty sure. Let's go check it out."

We climbed down out of the cab and approached the bike. I stood at the end of the driveway, my arms folded across my chest, and waited as Pete circled the bike. Finally, he reached out and touched the marred place on the seat. "Who would do this to my beautiful bike — my baby?"

"My guess is Hensley realized he needed to disguise it. But at least it's still in one piece."

He nodded. "True, true. And maybe..." He scratched at the red paint. "Maybe I can get this off with lacquer thinner without damaging what's underneath." He stood back and surveyed the bike again. "What I don't understand is why he put saddlebags on it. They ruin the sleek line."

"I'm not sure, but I think he planned to use it as a means of escape after he finished with me and Cindy." The thought made me shudder. "So what do you say we get out of here."

Pete straddled the Harley and reached for the key. "Well, I won't be riding this tonight."

"Oh?"

"No key." He dismounted and began searching all the compartments, even the small bag attached to the sissy bar. "Nothing. He must have it on him."

"Well we can't leave it here in case Hensley makes it back over to this side of the Warners."

"Damn straight we ain't leaving it here. There's gotta be a way to load it in the back of your truck."

I knew picking it up wasn't an option; it was much heavier that Pete's dirt bike. Looking around, I noticed the fortified banks of the Pit River. "Think we can push your motorcycle up there?" I asked, pointing to the mounds at the end of the street.

"Oh, yeah." He flashed his famous grin at me. "No problemo!" He worked on pushing the bike down the street while I backed the truck into position. Unfortunately, there still was a gap of a couple of feet between the top of the mound and the open tailgate. "Damn, now what!" I exclaimed, looking around for anything to use as a ramp.

"Let's look over there," Pete said, nodding at a shed at the back of Cindy's property.

We jumped the short fence and trotted over to the small building. Using the flashlight I'd retrieved from my front pocket, we quickly explored inside. Tucked behind an old-fashioned push mower and a handful of metal fence posts, we located a solid wooden door. Using that and a coil of clothesline we found hanging on the wall, the motorcycle was soon loaded into the truck and tied down.

I checked my watch; it was after nine, and thoughts of pork chops and gravy made my stomach growl. "Time to..." A huge yawn interrupted me. "... head back."

Pete grinned. "Looks like I better drive."

I nodded and climbed into the cab. My Dooley was less conducive to cuddling than the GTO, so I slipped off my long-sleeved shirt, rolled it up and used it for a pillow as I reclined against the passenger door. The last thing I remembered was turning off of Highway 395 and heading up the mountain toward the pass.

I know he's out there — waiting. It's dark — too dark to see. The road is winding, and the headlights are too dim. I try to slow down but I can't; the brakes aren't working, no matter how hard I push on the pedal. Suddenly, a gunshot explodes from nowhere...

Startled awake, I lunged against my seatbelt.

"Whoa there, Sarah!" Pete leaned across the center console, grasped my shoulders and gently pushed me back into my seat. "Take it easy. I didn't mean to startle you; just stopped by my place to grab my extra bike key."

"Just a bad dream; I'll be fine. Thanks." Determined not to continue it, I shifted in my seat while he started the truck and pulled out of his driveway. I focused on the road, knowing I'd soon be seated at Remy's kitchen table.

Thirty minutes later, the three of us were discussing the night's adventure and the ensuing manhunt.

"I don't think he's left the area," I said, drizzling a second ladle of gravy onto my plate. "Hensley doesn't give up that easily."

"If that's so, then I reckon you best stay here tonight," Remy said. "No tellin' if this fella knows where you live. At least here, me and Bessie can protect you."

"I'll stay too if it's okay with Remy," Pete added. "Slugger and I can hold our own."

"Look, I appreciate what you guys are trying to do." My eyes shifted from one man to the other. "But I'm perfectly capable of taking care of myself."

"No one's questioning that," Pete said, cutting his pork chop into bite-size pieces.

"That's right." Remy nodded once. "It's just that partners watch out for each other!"

Pete winked at me, and I had to smile. "Fine Remy, I'll stay."

A huge grin spread across his bearded face. "I'll make up the spare bed as soon as we finish supper."

"No need to go to all that trouble," I protested. "The couch will be just fine."

"Sorry, but that's my spot." Pete shrugged. "Guess you can have the recliner."

I glanced at Remy, but he pretended to be intensely interested in stirring gravy into his potatoes. Looking back at Pete, I wasn't surprised to find him similarly fascinated by arranging his green beans into some kind of design. "I give up! It's obvious the two of you are conspiring against me. Go ahead — make up the spare bed, but I call kitchen detail."

"And I'll help," Pete chimed in.

Remy laughed. "Fair enough."

By the time we had the table cleared and dishes done, Remy had gotten my bed ready and prepared a place on the couch for Pete. Millie and Bubbles, who had obediently stayed on their blanket during dinner, frolicked through the house, thoroughly investigating the increased activity.

"So what's the story behind the goat?" Pete asked, leaning against the counter and drying his hands on one of the many rooster-adorned kitchen towels. We watched as Millie leapt back and forth across Bubbles' back.

"I found it while I was patrolling around Eagleville. I thought it was one of those missing crias."

"Doesn't look like an alpaca to me."

I glared at him. "I didn't get a good look at it before I grabbed it. All I saw was a flash of white behind a big sagebrush."

"Oh, I see. So basically, you stole it." He turned away to hang the towel on the handle of the stove.

"I did not! I put up flyers everywhere, but no one has called me yet."

Laughing, he threw up his hands in surrender. "Okay, okay."

"All right you critters," Remy said as he came down the hallway toward the living room, "time for bed." The two small animals immediately halted and trotted over to him. He petted each head and pointed toward the folded blanket on the floor next to his recliner. Without another word, they went over and plopped down. Pete and I looked at each other; I shrugged and shook my head. "I'm turning in," Remy said, heading back down the hall. "Night."

"Probably a good thing no one has called to claim that goat," Pete whispered. "Doubt Remy'd give it up."

I smiled. "Well, if he wouldn't give up Buck, I'm pretty sure he won't give up Millie."

Pete cocked his head to one side. "Who's Buck?"

"The fawn."

"Fawn? What fawn?"

"Long story. I'll tell you later. Right now I'm going to bed, too. Goodnight." I left the kitchen and started down the hall with Bubbles close behind, leaving Pete to turn off the lights.

The spare bedroom was just that, a small room simply furnished with a double bed, nightstand, short dresser and an old upholstered chair. The light near the bed had been turned on and the covers were folded back, beckoning me to slip between the coolness of the sheets. Almost too tired to undress, I emptied my pockets, putting my phone, flashlight, and keys on the dresser. Then I unstrapped my ankle holster and placed the Kel-Tec .380 on the nightstand. Slowly I peeled off my clothes and draped them across the chair. My body armor was the last thing to come off, feeling much heavier than when I strapped it on. I'd just dropped it on the floor when my cell phone vibrated, causing me to jump at least six inches. Apprehensive, I plucked it off the dresser and flipped it open. It was a text from Cindy.

From: Cindy

just wanna say thnx. i shoulda listened to u.
dirk sez we'll get the guy but idk. i'm just so
scared. b careful.

Received: Wed Apr 29, 10:59pm

I hit the reply button and typed in my response.

To: Cindy

i'm glad it turned out ok. i'll be careful. got 2
bodyguards. lol

Sent: Wed Apr 29, 11:01pm

Then I snapped my phone shut and turned it off.
Snagging my T-shirt off the chair as I went by, I
tugged it on as I padded over to where Bubbles was
waiting. "Come on, Dog," I said, picking up the miniature mutt, "move over." I crawled into bed and set
him on the covers next to me. After circling a couple
of times, he plopped down, lowered his head to his
front paws, and closed his eyes.

Wishing I could fall asleep as easily, I lay on
my back and stared at the ceiling. *Where the hell
is Hensley?* With the vastness of the rugged, unin-
habited Warner wilderness, he could literally vanish
until he was ready to make his move. And he would.
Richard Hensley was not the type of man to give up
easily. After all, he'd staged his own death. Was
mine next?

Chapter 22

At the first sign of daybreak with barely enough light to make out the branches on the tree outside the window, I threw back the covers and abandoned the borrowed bed. Sleep had cruelly eluded me, and my brain was foggy with fatigue, but I had no choice. Hensley had to be found.

Determined to take advantage of every moment of daylight, I quickly dressed, made the bed, and headed out to the kitchen where I was greeted by the smell of fresh-brewed coffee and a retired carpenter. "Good morning," Remy said, fussing over something on the stove top.

"Morning." I reached for the coffee pot and filled a rooster mug, hoping the dose of caffeine would clear my head.

"Got some flapjacks here that are just about ready." He turned over the bubbly disks, to reveal their crispy, golden undersides.

"Thanks Remy, but I'm not hungry. Some coffee is all I need right now. Besides, I have to get out on patrol." Taking a cautious sip, I welcomed the burning sensation on my lips as it seemed to heighten my awareness. Then I dug my keys out of my pocket and slid the key to my Dooley off the ring. "I'll leave this in case Pete needs to reposition the truck to unload his bike," I said, placing it on the checkered tablecloth.

"Hold up a minute, and I'll drive you over there." Remy scooped the pancakes off the cast iron griddle and added them to the stack keeping warm in the oven.

"No need. It'll just take me a few minutes to walk home."

He shook his head. "No tellin' where that lunatic is by now. Me and Bessie are taking you home and that's that." He washed his hands and wiped them down the front of his green plaid shirt. "Besides, don't think Sleeping Beauty over there," he nodded toward Pete, "will be waking up for a while." We both turned and looked at the snoring figure asleep on the couch, buried under a colorful quilt and small goat that had curled up on his legs.

I chuckled. "I believe you're right. I'll get my stuff and meet you at the door." As I gathered my belongings, I realized how fortunate I was to have a friend who genuinely cared about my well-being, even if he was stubborn, overprotective, and sometimes a real pain in the ass. After making sure I hadn't left anything behind, I grabbed my body armor, threw it over my shoulder and headed back down the hall.

As Remy and I started for the door, Bubbles trotted over. "Not this time," I told him. "You stay here and guard the place." The tiny dog stared at me, as if considering his options, then slunk over to the couch and joined Millie on the human cushion. Remy grabbed his prized .45-70 from its place of honor along with his black felt hat, and we left.

"You can just drop me off by the corral," I said as

we pulled down my driveway in his Land Cruiser. "I need to feed Raven before showering and putting on my uniform."

"Nonsense," Remy said. "I'll take care of the horse whilst you get ready. This here's a better vantage point to keep an eye out for that fella." He parked next to my patrol unit and killed the engine. "You want me to go inside and give the place a quick look-see?"

"No thanks. I got it," I said as I opened the passenger door and slid out. I doubted Hensley had gotten anywhere near my place, especially stumbling around in the dark, but I had to admit what Remy had said made me slightly nervous.

As he strode toward the barn, his rifle swinging at his side, I headed for the house and began peeling off clothes the second I walked through the door. Ten minutes later, I'd had an invigorating cold shower and was standing in the middle of my bedroom, wearing my favorite robe and a towel wrapped around my head. I'd just started dressing when a loud thud came from the kitchen. "Remy, is that you?" No reply. Dressed in only a sports bra and briefs, I eased over to my bedside stand and grabbed my .38 Special. Then, as quietly as possible, I moved toward the kitchen.

As I eased around the corner of the stove, the crash of pans hitting the floor came from the pantry. My heart pounded as I crept past the fridge. I drew in a deep breath and leapt into the doorway, my gun grasped in both hands and held out in front of me. Without warning, something hurtled toward my face. I screamed, stumbled backward, and fired. Seconds later, Remy burst through the front door, slamming it into the wall and holding his rifle across his chest like a soldier on maneuvers.

"What in tarnation is going on in here?" he demanded.

Before I had the composure to answer, a huge ground squirrel scampered out from under the kitchen table, rushed between Remy's feet, and dashed out the door. We stared at each other for several seconds and then burst into laughter.

"Hells bells, where did that varmint come from?" he said, pulling off his felt hat, swiping at his brow with his sleeve, and replacing the hat.

I shook my head. "I have no idea." Glancing back into the pantry I added, "I guess it has been inside for a while." A box of cereal had been torn open, and its contents scattered on the floor. A loaf of bread was half-consumed, and a burst bag of flour gave everything a fine dusting of white. "Ugh, what a mess!"

"Uh, don't ya think you should finish gettin' dressed?" he said, removing his hat again and holding it in front of his face.

Realizing the scantiness of my outfit, I pulled the towel off my head and wrapped it around my torso. "Sorry, Remy," I muttered, retreating to my bedroom.

Moments later, I reemerged in full uniform, including my body armor. Wanting to be prepared for any surprises, I'd strapped on the Kel-Tac .380 as well as the .38 Special hidden in the shoulder holster under my jacket. Last thing, I fastened my gun belt around my waist, grabbed my cell phone, and walked out the front door.

Remy was seated in the Adirondack chair under

my apple tree with Bessie resting across its wooden arms. "All clear out here." He stood, and we headed toward the vehicles.

"Thanks Remy," I said, turning on my phone and shoving it into my pocket. It immediately went off, so I pulled it back out and noticed I had one missed call and a voicemail. Hoping it was good news about Hensley, I played the message. Instantly, my ear was bombarded by a cacophony of a man screaming, a dog barking, and hysterical crying. All I could make out was "...something terrible...come right away..." and then the call disconnected.

"Who was that?" Remy asked.

"No idea, but it sounded like all hell was busting loose."

"What if that fella's stirring up some kinda trouble?" He stepped toward my passenger door. "Maybe I should tag along as backup."

I shook my head. "Without knowing who that was, how would I know where to head?"

"Seems to me," he began, pushing his hat up with his free hand and scratching his head as he came around the front of my unit, "folks with them there cell phones can hit a button and call back whoever it was called them." Then he pulled on the brim of his hat and settled it into position.

I stared at him. *Why didn't I think of that?* Stress, lack of sleep, or distracted by a homicidal maniac? Or a combination of all three? Whatever the reason, I definitely was not operating at full capacity. "Yes Remy," I said, looking at the phone I still held in my hand, "of course I can." I hit the green button, and my phone sent the call. It was answered on the first ring.

"That you, Deputy?" Again a man's voice. "We need someone out here right away! It's terrible — Champ, get back..." Silence.

AHA! "It's Bob Robertson. I need to go." I climbed in behind the wheel and started the engine.

"Mind yourself," Remy called as I backed up.

Glancing in the rearview mirror as I sped off, I saw him fling his free arm in front of his face and spin around in an attempt to avoid the pelting of rocks thrown by my spinning tires. "Sorry Remy," I said again as I reached the pavement and accelerated toward County Road 1. I'd just cleared Fort Bidwell when my radio crackled.

"Unit 113, Modoc County."

Cindy! "Good to hear you, Modoc. Go ahead."

"Got a call from that alpaca rancher. Not sure what's going on. He just kept saying to send someone right away, and then the line went dead. I tried to reconnect but only got a busy signal. You don't think..."

"Copy that. Just keep trying. I'm on my way."

"Okay — I mean, copy 113. Time 5:54." *She sounds as rattled as I feel.*

Taking advantage of the early hour, I drove the narrow county road at interstate speed, diligently watching for equipment or livestock to cross my path. Except for swerving around an old beat up Pinto precariously parked along the last straightaway a quarter of a mile from my destination, the roads were clear, and I reached the ranch in just under twenty-five minutes. Pulling into the driveway, I noticed that the peculiar neighbor with the alien fixation and faded overalls had positioned himself near the fence. We exchanged nods as I passed by.

Continuing up the driveway, I located the rancher pacing back and forth. Champ, tethered to a sturdy fence post with a piece of thick rope, watched as his owner moved from one side of the yard to the other like a spectator at a tennis match. The moment the man noticed me, he hustled my way, waving frantically. After easing into what was becoming my own personal parking space, I turned on my portable radio, attached the mic to my left shoulder, and climbed out of my unit. Bob Robertson stood at the back of it, wringing his hands.

"It's terrible, just terrible!" he exclaimed as he led the way back to the house. "Had to tie Champ up to keep him away from it," he said, nodding toward the large dog, "but that wasn't the worst of it. She," he began as we rounded the corner of the house, "has been hysterical the whole time." He pointed to a sobbing woman sitting on a rough-hewn, wooden bench. She looked like a cat burglar dressed entirely in black and, although I couldn't see the face hidden behind her hands, I recognized the shock of neon pink hair poking out from under the stocking cap she had crammed on her head. *Lulu DeLoure!*

"What are you doing here?" I asked.

She leapt to her feet and hurried toward me. "Oh Deputy, I'm so glad you're here. It's..." Her voice hitched and tears formed in her eyes. "...horrible!" Then she burst into tears. "All I wanted was to take a few pictures," she wailed, "you know, for the article. I never expected to find..." She began crying harder and returned to her place on the bench.

Assuming I'd get no further information from Lulu, I turned back to the alpaca rancher. "What exactly happened here?"

Lynne Sella

"Well," he began, "I don't rightly know." He tugged on the brim of his John Deere ball cap and folded his arms across his chest. "I'm surprised her blood-curdling scream didn't wake the dead. It certainly made Champ raise the alarm. By the time I got my pants on and headed out the back door, he was chomping at the bit, wanting to get into the big field. That's when I spotted her," he jerked his chin toward Lulu, "hightailing it toward me from the pond. Soon as I opened the gate, Champ took off like a shot. After making sure she wasn't hurt, I went after the damn dog. Took pulling on his collar with both hands to get him back to the house. That's when I called you the first time. Got no answer so I called the Sheriff."

"Yeah, Dispatch informed me you'd called. Did she call you back?"

"No." He pulled his cell phone out of his shirt pocket, looked at it and put it back. "Damn thing died, and I haven't had a chance to plug it in."

"Okay." I stepped a few feet away and keyed my mic. "Modoc, 113."

"Go ahead 113, this is Modoc."

"I'm 10-20 but still not sure of the situation. Will let you know as soon as I find out."

"Copy 113. Time 6:30."

I moved back over to where the other two were waiting. "Okay Mr. Robertson, time to tell me what's going on."

He shook his head. "Better to show you." Then he started toward the gate that opened into the large field, and I fell in behind. As we got closer to the pond on the far end, I could tell there was some kind of form on the ground, but I couldn't quite make it out.

181

"Hope you got a strong stomach," he said as we continued walking. No sooner had he said that, I realized the form near the edge of the pond was the snake Pete and I had discovered a few days earlier. It was much larger than I had imagined and coiled around something. I immediately halted and put my hand on the rancher's arm. "Is it safe?"

"Oh I don't think it's going anywhere," he said, starting to walk toward it again. Seeing no other choice, I followed him.

Walking around the giant snake, the first thing I noticed was the military style boots at the end of a pair of legs wearing camouflage pants. A white T-shirt was visible through the coils of the snake's body, but the head and most of the left shoulder had been engulfed by the snake. A knife, grasped in the man's right hand, was stuck in the snake's body just behind its head, the tail end of a snake tattoo visible on the upper arm.

"Got no idea who this guy is or why he was in my field," Bob Robertson said, standing with his arms again folded across his chest, "but he sure got the surprise of his life."

"Yeah, he sure did," I muttered. Pressing the transceiver button on the mic I called in. "Modoc, this is 113. I have an 11-44 at my location." My stomach clenched, and the ground started to slowly spin. My field of vision diminished in size and brightness, and there was a ringing in my ears. As I felt myself leaning too far to one side, a pair of strong hands gripped both my arms just above the elbow and held me upright.

"You all right, Deputy?" Bob Robertson asked, his face only inches from mine.

"Yeah I'm fine," I said, shaking my head in an attempt to clear it. "Just a little dizzy." He released me and stepped back. That's when my cell phone went off. Grateful for the distraction, I pulled it out and answered. "Murdock."

"Is it him?"

Her question caught me off-guard, so it took a moment to realize it was Cindy and respond. "Yes."

An audible sigh came over the line. "I'll get the meat wagon rolling."

"Uh, you might send an extra deputy and maybe a Sawzall."

"A Sawzall! What for?"

"Well," I began, "you see..." Not sure how else to answer her I blurted, "The snake got him!"

This time it was a sharp intake of air on the other end. "Oh dear," she muttered and then disconnected.

"Sounds like you know who this here fella is," the rancher said.

"Yeah, that's right." I walked around the gruesome form one more time. "I know exactly who this is."

Chapter 23

My legs were still a bit shaky as I walked back to the Explorer to retrieve my camera. Anxious to wrap up the recovery of Hensley's body as quickly as possible, I figured snapping pictures of the scene while waiting for the coroner's van would speed up the process. As I opened the back of my unit, I realized Lulu DeLoure had followed me.

"I'm really sorry I didn't listen to you," she said. "I didn't think it would hurt to sneak in, take a few pictures, and then sneak out." She ran the fingers of her right hand up and down the camera strap she wore around her neck. "I never in my wildest dreams thought I'd find..." Her voice trailed off, and she shuddered. "What's gonna happen now?"

"Well, I need to take pictures to document the scene," I said, grabbing my evidence case and opening it, "before they get here to load up the body." I pushed the power button on my camera but nothing happened. I popped open the small compartment on the bottom, dumped out the batteries, and dug around in my case for some replacements but found only one. "Damn!"

"What's wrong?" she asked.

"My camera is out of commission." I stuffed it

back into my case and closed the rear door. "You think I could borrow yours?" I asked, pointing to the digital camera she had hanging around her neck.

"Well, I don't know..."

"You let me use it, and I'll let you report on the recovery."

"You mean I can watch and take pictures and everything? Like an exclusive?"

"Absolutely," I said, trying not to smile.

"This could show my editor I'm ready to be a real reporter!" She pulled the strap over her head and thrust the camera into my hands. "I'm going to need my notebook. I'll be right back." Then she ran down the driveway, turned left and ran down the road until she disappeared from sight. I shook my head and started back toward the large field.

"You look like you're feeling better," Bob Robertson said as we reached the gate simultaneously.

"Yeah I am, thanks. Where'd you put the dog?" I asked, noticing the animal was no longer tied to the post.

"Oh, I put him in the barn. Figured we didn't need him causing a raucous when folks arrive to clean up that mess."

I nodded. "Probably a good idea. Speaking of cleaning up, is there another way into this field with an opening big enough to drive a van through?"

"Nope. This here's the only way in." He jerked his thumb at the gate next to us. "And no way I'm cutting a hole in my fence," he said, anticipating my next question. "This fiasco has cost me enough already."

I nodded again. "Okay."

"But," he began, "I may have a way to haul that

guy outta here. Got a trailer I tow with my four-wheeler that fits through this gate. Just might do the trick."

"I think you're right. Do you mind getting it hooked up and ready to go? But leave it parked near the driveway, and we can use it to haul in the equipment we'll need."

"You got it." And he took off toward the barn.

Taking a deep breath, I pushed through the gate and walked toward the pond. When I got close enough, I turned on Lulu's camera and began taking photos. Even though it was a little easier to handle not seeing Henley's face, I finished as quickly as I could and headed back.

By the time I walked across the field and made the turn around the corner of the house, the driveway looked like a parking lot. At least eight more cars, including the old Pinto I'd had to swerve around on the way there, were haphazardly parked, completely blocking the driveway, and their drivers were milling around.

"Excuse me folks," I called as I approached, "you'll need to move your vehicles back out onto the road, please. We need to clear this area for emergency vehicles."

The crowd stopped, looked at me, and then continued to move about, talking with each other. *Unbelievable!*

I tried again. "Folks, if I could have your attention." But no one even looked my way that time until the trunk lid on the dilapidated Pinto parked behind me slammed shut, and I jumped like I'd been shot. Then everyone stared.

"Oh Deputy, I'm so sorry," Lulu said as she

stepped away from what I assumed was her vehicle. She had swapped her black stocking cap for her red-rimmed glasses with the oversized lenses, which still clashed with her hair. "I didn't mean to startle you."

"Oh, that's okay. You..."

"All right you people," she shouted at the crowd as she moved toward them, "you heard the Deputy. Get this area cleared out. I've got this story covered, and you all can read about what happened next week when the newspaper comes out."

Again the crowd hesitated and stared at Lulu, who was waving her hands over her head. But they didn't actually disperse until Bob Robertson appeared and told them to clear off his property. The last car had just pulled out when the coroner's van arrived. Hoping to avoid another traffic jam, I positioned Lulu at the end of the driveway with instructions to let no one through and then went to help unload the van.

"You guys are not going to believe this," I said as I walked around to the back of the van and found myself face-to-face with Sandusky. "What are you doing here?"

"Finishing what we started last night. I wanna see for myself that it's this Archie guy."

"Hensley," I corrected.

"Whatever. Now where is he?"

"In this big field to the back, over by the pond. We can't drive in there, but the rancher has a four-wheeler and trailer we can use to haul in our stuff and haul out the body. Did you bring the Sawzall?"

"Sure did, but I still don't get why," Josh Green

said as he stepped from the side door of the van, the cutting tool in his hands.

"You'll see," I said. "And you might want to grab a utility jumpsuit and some goggles too."

We had most of the equipment, including the Stokes litter, loaded onto the trailer when a heated argument erupted at the end of the driveway. Glancing that way, I recognized Remy's Land Cruiser and I took off running. *Will it ever end?*

"I told you no one is allowed in here," Lulu shouted as I got close enough to make out what was being said. She and Remy were standing toe-to-toe, their faces only inches apart.

"And I told you I'm not some riffraff off the street," he shouted back, his fists pressed to his waist and his elbows out. "I'm her damn partner!"

Pete, who was leaning against the front of the rig, had his arms folded across his chest and a huge grin on his face.

"Lulu, it's okay," I gasped. "They're clear to come in, and we're about ready to get started." I took a couple deep breaths. "Your camera is on the trailer with the other equipment. Remy, why don't you leave the Toyota where it is. It can be our barrier."

They gave each other a curt nod, as if to say I-told-you-so and proceeded up the driveway. Pete winked at me, and we followed along behind.

"What was all the commotion, Murdock?" Sandusky asked when I returned to the van.

"Just a misunderstanding," I said.

"And who are all these people?" he continued.

"Lulu DeLoure is the reporter who found the body, sir." She smiled and did a little finger wave. *Good grief!* "And this is Remy Hamilton and Pete

Yarbrough. They were at the church last night, remember?"

"So why are they here now?"

"Probably for the same reason you are — to make sure it's Hensley." The man was beginning to infuriate me.

"Well, this is official business and…"

I cut him off. "And I'm sure we're going to need their help."

The Undersheriff glared at me, but I just glared back. I was in no mood for his macho bullshit. Finally he said, "Just make sure they stay out of the way." Then he nodded at Bob Robertson to fire up the four-wheeler, and we headed into the field.

"Holy cow!" Josh said as he made his third trip around the snake-wrapped body. "This is incredible!"

"You're sure this is that Archie guy?"

"Hensley, and yeah. That's what he was wearing and see this?" I pointed to the snake tattoo that ran up his arm and disappeared inside the huge reptile's mouth. "Both Pete and I can identify him by this."

Pete stepped closer. "Yep, that's definitely the guy that was with Cindy at Lenny's place."

"Good," Sandusky said. "Now that we've got a positive ID, let's get this loaded up and hauled outta here."

As he and Josh began setting up the litter, I moved closer to Remy and Pete. "Aren't you glad I coaxed you to let go of that thing the other day?" I said, nudging Pete with my elbow.

"Sure am. Had no idea it was that big."

"What kind of snake is that?" Remy asked.

"Python maybe," Pete said, "but I'm not sure."

"Green anaconda." Both Pete and Remy turned

and stared at me. "What? Cindy found out yesterday morning that it was stolen from the Las Vegas
Zoo."

"Well looks to me like that fella put up quite a
fight," Remy said. "But how the hell did he end up
in here?"

"I've been wondering that myself," I said.

"Pretty sure he didn't go through the gate or I'd've
known it," Bob Robertson said, joining us. "Champ
was in the small field and would've started barking
if anyone came down the driveway."

"I can show you how I got in if you like," Lulu offered as she passed by.

"You didn't get in through the gate either?" I
asked.

She shook her head. "The plan was to come along
the fence, take a few pictures and leave. But the willows blocked most of the pond, so I..."

"This thing isn't budging at all," Josh exclaimed,
tugging on the coils around Hensley's legs. He
straightened up and walked around it again. "How
are we gonna get it off?"

"Sawzall," I replied. The rest of the group looked
at me as if I was crazy, but I continued. "If you cut
a big chunk out of each coil," I said, moving closer
and holding my hands approximately two feet apart,
"we should be able to pull the body out."

"Yeah, that just might work," Josh said "But
what about this?" He pointed to where the snake's
head had enveloped Hensley's. "I'm not sure we'll be
able to pull this part off."

"Doubtful." Pete stepped forward. "The teeth are
angled in such a way that any attempt to pull something out of its mouth only sinks them in deeper."

"And what are you?" Sandusky asked. "Some kinda expert?"

Here we go! "Yes, actually he is," I retorted.

He stood off to the side, his arms folded across his chest and a scowl on his face. "Hmph," he said, dropping his hands to his sides and stepping over to the trailer. "Then cut off the head and let the guys in Redding deal with it."

"Cut off the guy's head?" Josh asked, his eyes widening bigger than the lenses of his glasses.

Lulu gasped.

"No you idiot, the snake's head." Sandusky picked up the utility jumpsuit and flung it at Josh. "Now get going! Don't plan on being here all damn day."

The young lab technician muttered something as he unrolled the suit. I couldn't make it out and hoped Sandusky couldn't either.

"Would you mind showing me how you got into the field?" I asked Lulu, taking the opportunity to avoid the disassembly of the dead snake.

Her gaze shifted from Josh to me and back again. "Uh, sure but let's hurry, so I don't miss anything." As she led the way to the corner of the field, I found it difficult to believe this was the same woman who'd been hysterically sobbing earlier.

"This is where I climbed the fence," she said when we finally reached the corner. "I held onto the wire, stuck my toes through the holes of the fencing, and walked up this big slanted post."

"You grabbed this top wire?" I asked.

"Yeah, why?"

Slowly, I reached my hand toward the hot wire that ran along the top of the no-climb fencing, anticipating a sudden surge of electricity as soon as I touched it, but nothing happened. Not one spark. "Then what?" I asked, letting go and moving back.

"When I got close to the top, I stepped over the fence and climbed down the post on the other side." Just then Josh fired up the gas-powered Sawzall. "Oh, I need to get back. Don't want to miss anything." She scurried around the willows and dashed back to the group huddled in the field.

After studying the railroad tie Lulu had climbed on, I inspected the adjacent one. Small splinters had been scuffed off along the outside edge and sections of that area of fence had been bent out of shape as if someone had pulled on it. Hensley had definitely gotten into the field the same way as Lulu.

By the time I rejoined the recovery effort, Josh had reduced the giant snake to a pile of large reptile chunks, and the men were wrestling the body bag into the litter and then onto the trailer while Lulu circled, snapping pictures. "So what do we do with the leftovers?" Josh asked shrugging out of the jumpsuit.

"Leave it," Sandusky said. "Buzzards gotta eat."

"You can't leave that here," Bob Robertson exclaimed. "I need to move my animals back into this field. They've been in the barn too long as it is."

"That reminds me," I said, addressing the rancher. "When did you shut down the hot wire on this field?"

"The hot wire?" He didn't turn but continued to watch as Josh loaded the last of the equipment onto the trailer. "Well, I moved my alpacas the day I discovered that damn snake. What was that? Tuesday?

That's when I cut the electricity to it." He finally faced me. "Why?"

"That explains how Hensley and Lulu were able to get into the field by climbing your fence."

"You mean if I hadn't turned the juice off, this man might still be alive?" He frowned as he nodded toward the bulging black bag waiting on the trailer.

"Possibly." *And hunting me!!* "You can't blame yourself. You had no way of knowing anyone was going to jump over your fence and get eaten by the giant snake that had somehow made its way into your pond." The expression on the rancher's face did not change. "For what it's worth, he was a wanted man and considered armed and dangerous," I offered.

"He was?" He raised both eyebrows. "Well then..."

"All right," Sandusky called. "Time to go, so let's get a move on."

Lulu snapped the lens cap back onto her camera. "I'll make sure you get a set of prints. I'll leave them at the front desk for you." Then she bolted from the field.

Pete checked his watch. "Oh man, I need to get to the Spur. Gotta clean up from last night and stock the bar." He leaned in closer. "Stop by on your way home, and I'll buy you a cold one." Flashing me that grin of his, he called to Remy, "Ready to go?"

"Yeah. Gotta few chores of my own to get done."

I had to smile as the two of them strolled across the field and through the gate. They had become quite chummy in the last couple of days, and for some unknown reason that made me nervous.

"You gonna drive this thing outta here or should I have Josh here do it?" Sandusky demanded.

"I'm coming," Bob Robertson said as he hustled

over to where the Undersheriff was waiting, "but I must insist you do something about that snake."

"The Sheriff's Office isn't in the habit of removing dead animals," Sandusky said. "Perhaps, if you contact Fish and Game or the BLM, they can help you."

I moved closer, hoping to reason with Dirk the Jerk when my radio went off. "113, Modoc County."

I reached up and pressed the transceiver button on the mic near my left ear. "Modoc, this is 113."

"Just got off the phone with the Las Vegas Zoo. They'll be here tomorrow to pick up the snake for examination and have requested that we secure it and hold it in cold storage."

Good old Cindy. "Copy." As I looked at Sandusky, I wasn't surprised to see the color of his face deepen and his eyes narrow to fine slits.

"Son-of-a-bitch!" he exclaimed. "Josh, we're gonna need another damn body bag."

Chapter 24

The coroner's van barely paused before turning left onto County Road 1 and heading north. Having to secure the remains of the giant snake had extended the recovery time by almost an hour, and Sandusky's mood had grown more sour with each passing minute. At least I'd managed to pull Josh aside and ask him to check Hensley's pockets for a motorcycle key and possibly a cell phone before the body was sent on to Redding, explaining the situation involving Pete's stolen motorcycle. Then I'd wished him good luck on his ride back to the office with Sandusky.

I left as Bob Robertson began ushering the females and their young out of the barn and back into the large field. As I reached the end of the driveway, I smiled and waved at the neighbor who was still loitering there. He returned the gesture before walking away. Driving through Cedarville, I decided I could use a large cup of extra strong coffee from the Wagon Wheel, so I parked in front and went inside.

"What'll you have, Deputy?" the waitress asked as I sat down at the counter.

"No need to be so formal, Sal. Call me Sarah."

I plucked a menu from the metal rack more from habit than necessity.

"Don't seem fittin' while you're in uniform, Hon."

"Okay," I said, suppressing a chuckle. "I need an extra-large coffee with cream and sugar, please." I closed the menu and replaced it in the rack.

Sal frowned at me. "Sure you don't want something more substantial?"

"No time. I need to get back to the office and take care of some paperwork."

"Alrighty then. One cup of joe comin' up." She stepped over to the double pot coffee maker and filled a milkshake-sized Styrofoam cup with the black brew, added a three-second stream from the sugar dispenser and topped it off with half-and-half from a carton she pulled out of the mini-fridge under the counter. Then she snapped on the lid and brought it to me. "Here you go, Deputy. This ought to get you through 'til lunchtime."

"Thanks, Sal, What do I owe you?"

"On the house." She retreated into the kitchen before I could protest, so I pulled three singles out of my pocket and left them on the counter, letting her determine whether they would go toward the tab or the tip jar. Thirty minutes later I arrived at the Sheriff's Office, my coffee gone and only a vague recollection of driving over the pass, and headed straight for the bathroom.

I came out just in time to see Josh and three deputies pushing through the double doors that led to the adjacent county jail, struggling under the weight of a dismantled snake zipped inside the body bag.

"Where are you going with that?" I asked.

"Sandusky wants it stashed in the walk-in behind

the jail," Josh said between grunts, his glasses slowly sliding down his nose.

"Where is Sandusky?" Avoiding him was definitely a good idea.

"Lining Ira out for the trip to Redding," he said just before the foursome disappeared through the doors.

"Lucky Ira," I murmured as I headed for the dispatch desk. As I rounded the corner, I was startled to see the welt on the side of Cindy's face had transformed into a fairly large bruise. "Oh man, that looks like it hurts."

Her hand immediately touched the spot. "Guess it could have been worse, huh?"

I nodded. "Much worse. No telling what that bastard had in mind."

"Yeah." She paused, and her eyes filled with tears. "I just feel so stupid, falling for his bullshit!"

"I understand exactly what you mean. I'm still trying to figure out how I didn't recognize him." We stared at each other for a few seconds, sharing a mutual misperception.

"Well, I better get started on my report before Sandusky gets on my case. I'm sure it will take a while." Then I retreated into the small conference room across the hall from the break room and fired up one of the computers. As it loaded, I pulled out my notebook and reviewed what few notes I'd written. Finding them rather sparse, I quickly jotted down what I remembered, starting with the phone call I'd received while having dinner at Remy's. By the time the computer was ready, I'd written over ten pages of notes, and I was ready to begin.

When I emerged over an hour later, my eyes felt

gritty, my back was stiff, and I had to get rid of the rest of my coffee. Having completed most of the report, I needed to verify some details captured in the pictures I'd taken but couldn't ignore my rumbling stomach any longer. I exited the bathroom and started toward the front of the building. Josh called to me as I passed the open door of the lab.

"Got something for you," he said after I'd spun around and returned to the doorway. He handed over a single key and a cell phone resembling a miniature BlackBerry.

"Great." I slid them into my front pants pocket. "Pete will be real glad to get these back."

"I took pictures of them to leave in the evidence box, but since the case is closed, I didn't see any reason for them to sit on a shelf indefinitely."

"Did you find anything else on him?" I was curious to see how far Hensley had taken this new identity thing.

"Funny you should ask." He moved over to one of the wide counters lining the walls. "I pulled off his belt in order to remove the knife sheath and pried the knife free from his hand. I even pulled off his boots in case he had something stashed in them but — nothing." He motioned to the items he had lined up on the counter; a rolled up black leather belt, the Buck knife Hensley had made me use to cut Cindy loose, the sheath he'd pulled it from, the military boots he'd worn, and the handgun Sandusky had picked up when he knocked Hensley over the head. "The guy had no wallet, no money, and no ID of any kind. Pretty weird if you ask me."

I shook my head. "You have no idea." I pointed at the gun. "So what was he carrying?"

"Smith and Wesson 40 caliber." He picked it up, ejected the magazine, and pulled back the slide before handing it to me. "It's one of their new lightweight, concealable pistols." The gun was much smaller and slimmer than the Ruger .357 Hensley was known to carry.

"Much easier to hide than his old handgun would've been." I handed it back. "Thanks again for the key and phone. I owe you one." He smiled at me, and I once again headed for the front of the building. As I neared the end of the hallway, I heard voices speaking in hushed tones. Peering around the corner, I was rather surprised to see Sandusky and Cindy leaning over the counter, their heads pressed together. Seemingly oblivious to their surroundings, I darted back into the hallway and waited.

Seconds ticked by until finally the Undersheriff whipped around corner and down the hall. "Skulking again, Murdock?" was all he said before disappearing into his office.

"Dirk the Jerk really pisses me off," I complained to Cindy as I approached her desk.

"Must you call him that?" She frowned at me.

"Since when do you care what people call Sandusky." She whirled around and glared at me; that's when I knew. "You've fallen for him, haven't you?"

"No I haven't *fallen* for him."

An incoming call interrupted her. "Modoc, this is 104."

Cindy sat in her chair, spun into position, and picked up her mic. "Go ahead, 104."

"Yeah, I'm Code 7"

"Copy 104. Time 11:22" She turned her chair to face me and crossed her arms in front of her chest.

"Look, it's not like I just met Dirk. I've known him for a long time."

I leaned on the counter. "And in that time have you ever considered him 'date' material?" I asked, using my fingers to make quotation marks in the air.

"Well, no..."

"They say that people who have shared some kind of traumatic event sometimes think they're in love."

"It's not like that." She stood and moved over closer. "Neither of us could sleep last night, so we sat up talking for hours. I know things about him now — things that explain why he is the way he is. And..." She leaned closer and smiled. "We actually have things in common, but I never realized how much."

"Really?" My stomach growled again. "How about we go grab some lunch and continue this conversation."

"Uh, well..." She looked down. "You see, I mean..."

"You and Sandusky?"

She nodded. "He just asked me to lunch before you got here. I'm sorry."

"That's okay," I told her. "I've got things to do anyway. We can go some other time. I'll see you later." I'd almost reached the front door when I thought of something. "Hey Cindy," I called as I turned around. "Did Hensley leave anything in your car?"

She stared at me longer than I'd expected. "I don't think so," she finally said, slowly shaking her head.

"Well, when you get a chance would you mind checking?"

"Sure, I'll check when we get back from lunch. What are you looking for?"

"To be honest, I don't really know." Then I pushed through the glass door and headed for my vehicle. As I pulled out onto the highway, an unusual feeling of melancholy washed over me like a huge wave. But why? It wasn't like I had latent feelings for Hensley. Our short-lived relationship had been over for quite a while, and the last time we worked together his arrogance had almost caused me to sacrifice my integrity. And so what if Cindy was drawn to Sandusky. *If he makes her happy, isn't that all that matters?* But still the feeling persisted. Maybe it wasn't Hensley so much but the part of my life he represented.

Deciding I needed comfort food for lunch, I headed south on Main Street to the hamburger joint on the outskirts of town. After ordering a double bacon-cheeseburger, a large order of fries and a chocolate malt, I sat in the exact spot I'd occupied a few months ago when I was considering a change in my career. Sue James told me I was making a terrible mistake, and there were times when I thought she was probably right. But Modoc County had become home for me and..."Sue!"

"No ma'am, my name's Barbie. Here's your order," she said, placing a tray on the table and sliding it in front of me. "Need anything else?"

"Uh, no. I think I'm good. Thanks." The teenage waitress left, and I popped a french fry into my mouth before pulling out my cell phone and punching in Sue's number at the FBI. She picked up on the third ring.

"Federal Bureau of investigation, Art Crime Team."

"Hi Sue, it's Sarah."

"Hey Sarah, how the heck are you?"

Until I heard her voice, I hadn't realized how much I'd actually missed her. "I'm okay but I've been betta," I said, mimicking her Bostonian accent.

"Oh you're so funny, not. Seriously, whatsa matta with..." She paused. "Hensley! Is it Hensley?"

"Yeah," I murmured.

"Oh, Sarah! Are you all right? What happened?"

In between sips of my malt and an occasional french fry, I shared with Sue the sequence of events that had taken place over the past couple of weeks, ending with the discovery of Hensley's body encircled by the coils of a giant green anaconda.

"What a bastid! He certainly got what he deserved! I'm just so relieved you're okay."

"Me too. I'm not sure what he had in mind, but it probably wasn't good."

"Damn! I have to run — gotta meeting in a few minutes. Call me lata', okay?"

"Sure thing. Have fun!"

"Oh yeah, laugh a minute. Chow."

I snapped my phone shut and set it on the table next to my tray of food. Then I picked up the double-cheeseburger and did my best to imitate a Carl's Jr. commercial, complete with ketchup splotches on my uniform shirt, but I didn't care. My mind was focused on my meal and nothing else until the burger and most of my fries were gone. Feeling better, I was anxious to finish my report and put the whole Hensley thing behind me, so I wiped off my shirt as best I could with a handful of napkins and walked a couple of blocks north on Main Street to the newspaper office. As I approached the business counter, I recognized the two girls I'd encountered the last time I was there.

"Oh hello Deputy," the taller one said. "How can we help you today?"

"Miss DeLoure was supposed to leave something for me."

The shorter girl reached under the counter and retrieved a large manila envelope. "I think this is what you're looking for," she said, handing it over.

I opened the flap and pulled out a stack of photos. As I flipped through them, the taller girl leaned closer, craning her neck.

"Is that a snake?" she exclaimed.

I shoved the stack back into the envelope and started for the door, "Tell Miss DeLoure I said thank you."

"I told you we should have peeked at what was inside," the shorter girl hissed as she smacked the other girl's arm with the back of her hand. Suppressing a chuckle, I headed back down Main to my patrol unit.

Having returned to the office, I again sequestered myself in the small conference room, plugged in my flash drive, and opened my report. I spread the pictures on the large table and studied them for the missing details and soon had my report printed and ready to submit.

As I headed down the hall, Sandusky emerged from his office. "Murdock, what'd you find at that nutjob's motel room?"

Hensley's motel room! "On my way now, sir." I rolled up my report and gripped it like a relay baton. "Just making a pit stop," I said, pointing toward the ladies' room. I continued down the hall and pushed through the bathroom door. "Ugh!! How could I have spaced on his motel room?" I asked my reflection in the mirror over the row of sinks.

"Sarah?"

I whirled around and realized one of the stall doors was closed. *Good grief!* "Yeah, it's me."

"Is everything all right?"

"Everything's fine. I just came in to...uh..." I looked at my rolled up report I still held in my hand. "Just needed to throw something away." I shoved the report into the white metal garbage can that had on at least one occasion been the target of anger aimed at Sandusky. "See you later Cindy," I said, yanking the door open. Stepping into the hallway, I ran into Ira Fielding and knocked the clipboard he was carrying to the floor.

"Oh Ira, I'm so sorry," I stammered, reaching out to steady him on his feet. "How are you feeling?" I quickly scooped up the mess of paperwork and handed it back to him.

"A little better, I guess," he said in a hoarse, gravelly voice.

"That's good. Say did Sandusky give you any special instructions to pass on regarding contact with the FBI once a positive ID had been officially established?"

"Uh, I don't think so." He shuffled through the disarray of papers. "I don't see anything."

"Okay, thanks."

"Wel — " A sneeze exploded out of him. " — come." Then he turned and headed for the offloading room.

Unbelievable! The Undersheriff can be so exasperating! I debated on whether to bring it up, but the Bureau needed official notification, so I walked back up the hallway and knocked on his door.

"Enter."

I slowly opened the door and peered inside. "Undersheriff Sandusky?"

He barely glanced my way. "What now, Murdock?"

"I was wondering if you'd informed the FBI of Hensley's current status. I'm sure the deputy director — "

"Telling me how to do my job again?" Sandusky interrupted, volume and pitch both increased.

"No sir, I just wanted — "

"To quote me more regulations of you precious FBI?" His voice louder and dripping with sarcasm.

I stepped further into his office. "Look Sandusky," I said, extending my hands from my sides, palms up.

"Undersheriff!" he yelled. "Undersheriff Sandusky!" He leapt to his feet, crashing his chair into the bookshelf behind his desk and pointing toward the door. "Now, get out!"

I spun around, strode back into the hallway and slammed the door behind me. *That went well!*

Chapter 25

Driving into the Stony Ridge Motor Lodge is like traveling back in time. The vintage U-shaped building, with its manicured lawn and weedless flowerbeds filled with perennials, has been meticulously maintained for decades. And the rooms have not lost their charm, in spite of the addition of modern conveniences like miniature microwaves and refrigerators and bulky televisions. Staying there is like escaping the fast-paced world of today and exchanging it for the easier existence of long ago.

As I climbed out of my rig, Bert Evans strolled through the front door of the large living quarters adjacent to the tiny office.

"Howdy Sarah. What brings you to our little neck of the woods?"

"Hi, Bert. Wrapping up an investigation, but I didn't expect to find you here." I moved to the front of the Explorer.

"Came home for some lunch. Whatcha investigating?"

"Actually, it involves one of your long-term guests."

"Oh? Who's that?" He stepped off the small porch and leaned his substantial torso across my hood.

"You knew him as Archie Duncan."

"Well, I'm not surprised. Why just the other day — whaddya mean I knew him as Archie Duncan? That ain't his name?" His eyes narrowed.

I pushed my sunglasses up onto the top of my head like a headband and looked the large man in the eye. "His name was Richard Hensley, and he was wanted by the FBI for murder."

Bert snapped to attention. "That son-of-a-bitch. Always had a bad feeling about that guy, and when I see him I'm gonna teach him a thing or two!"

I shook my head. "Don't think so. He kind of had an accident."

"What kinda accident?"

"Let me into his motel room, and I'll fill you in."

"You got yourself a deal." He entered the small office and quickly returned, holding a large wad of keys. As we followed the driveway along the inside edge of the building, I explained the sequence of events that had taken place over the past few days, ending with Hensley's encounter with the giant snake. "And so you think it was that fella I helped haul up outta the creek bed that was responsible for letting that snake out, huh?"

"Yeah. Apparently it was stolen from the Las Vegas Zoo, but I'm not sure how he ended up with it or where he was taking it."

"Well, here we are," Bert said when we reached the door of Room 12 in the far southwest corner of the motor lodge. "Just like old times." It seemed odd to be standing outside the room I'd called home not so long ago, hoping to discover clues of a man I thought I knew. Bert inserted the key, unlocked the door, and stepped back.

At first, I didn't notice anything out of the ordinary. A few clothes hung from the small rack attached to the wall, and scaled-down versions of basic toiletries littered the narrow counter in the bathroom. Opening the fridge, I wasn't surprised to find a couple of take-out boxes and a partial six-pack of Budweiser.

"Well, would you look at this." Bert had followed me inside and was looking at a rather large picture hanging over the low dresser. The picture itself had been covered with a map of Surprise Valley and photographs were stuck around its perimeter.

"Omigod," I said, as my eyes moved from one photograph to the next; my parents' house in Red Bluff, the Sheriff's Office in Alturas, Remy's house, my house, the Silver Spur Saloon, the church in Eagleville where he'd taken Cindy, and even of me in my patrol unit at several different locations. "Where did these come from?"

Bert slid open the top drawer of the dresser, revealing a small digital camera, red Sharpie marker, roll of clear tape, a charge cord, and an open package of cable ties. "My guess is he took them there pictures himself." He checked his watch. "Well, I gotta get back to the tire shop. Let me know if you need anything else." Then he left me alone to finish searching the rest of the room, but I couldn't stop staring at the photographs.

I figured Hensley had been stalking me, but he'd also been watching my family and friends as well. The other photos had been taken of an old abandoned mine north of Fort Bidwell. The building that had once covered the shaft was in ruins, exposing the mouth of the deep pit.

Studying the map, I noticed red Xs at various locations; my house, the church in Eagleville, and a spot I was fairly certain was the abandoned mine. That X had a red circle around it, and my stomach clenched. I dropped into the nearest chair, the realization of what Hensley had planned washing over me. *The son-of-a-bitch was crazy!*

Suddenly, I was ready to be done with the whole Hensley thing. I began emptying the drawers, lining up the contents on the foot of the bed. Besides the camera and the other items from the top drawer, there were socks, underwear, and a few tank tops of various colors. At the back of the bottom drawer, I found an old ragged backpack rolled up around something heavy inside. I unrolled it and dumped out a box of ammo for the Smith & Wesson Shield 40 caliber handgun. A thorough search of its other compartments came up empty. I moved to the head of the bed and pulled open the drawer of the single nightstand, revealing a notepad and pen with the name of the motel stamped on them and the standard Gideon Bible. After flipping through the pages and finding nothing, I knew I needed help taking the place apart.

I punched the number to the office into my phone and interrupted Cindy before she'd gotten to the third word of her standard greeting. "Hey Cindy, it's Sarah. Patch me through to Josh would you?"

"Sure. Hang on."

It rang three times before he answered. "Lab. This is Josh."

"It's Sarah. How'd you like to do some more field work?"

"No way! I'm still picking bits of reptile outta my hair."

"Nothing as messy as that. I just need some help baggin' and taggin' the guy's motel room. I've given it a preliminary search but haven't located any kind of identification. Thought a second pair of eyes couldn't hurt."

"Okay. Where am I going, and how many evidence boxes should I bring?"

"Stony Ridge number twelve and three should do it."

"Got it. Be there in a few."

I snapped my phone shut and began pulling clothes off the rack. I recognized the cargo pants and short-sleeve shirts I'd seen Hensley wear as Archie Duncan as well as the tan loafers. The one article of clothing I couldn't recall ever seeing him wear was a green army coat I found hanging under one of the shirts. A thorough search of all the pockets, however, revealed nothing.

Next I stepped into the bathroom and scooped everything off the counter into the small, empty garbage can, which I added to the line of stuff on the foot of the bed. I was just about to get started on the mini-fridge when Josh showed up.

"Well?" he asked as he pushed through the door, hauling three cardboard evidence boxes.

"Well what?"

"Find anything good yet?"

I chuckled. "No."

"Bet I have something you'll be interested in." He dropped the boxes on the floor next to the bed, popped the lid off one of them, pulled out a large Ziploc bag and held it out toward me.

"What's this?" I opened it and looked inside.

"Cindy found that stuff under the driver's seat of her car. Figured you'd like to see it right away."

Upending the bag, a full clip for the handgun, a key to the motel room, and a camo-colored, nylon wallet tumbled out onto the bed. "Have you opened this?" I asked, picking up the wallet and tugging the Velcro fastener apart.

"Nope, thought I'd give you that honor."

Inside I found sixty-two dollars in mostly fives and tens along with a Maryland driver's license. I slid it out of the clear ID slot to get a better look.

"Is that what you were looking for?" Josh asked.

"Not exactly." I held out the identification.

"John Morgan? I thought this guy's name was Hensley."

"It is."

"So who's this Morgan guy and why would our dead guy have his license?"

I shook my head. "I have no clue. John Morgan worked under Hensley at the FBI, and as far as I know, he still works there. Why he would want his license?" Then I studied the blond hair and dark eyes in the photo. I had rarely seen John Morgan without the standard badass sunglasses he usually wore, but as I looked at his face, it was uncanny how much the two men resembled each other, even though Hensley had much darker hair and startling yellowish green eyes. Again I wondered how I hadn't recognized the man when I first saw him. Finally it dawned on me. "Unless..." I picked up the garbage can from the bathroom and emptied it onto the bed. Poking through the tiny toiletries, I came across what I'd initially believed to be some kind of medication in a foil packet. Turning it over, I discovered it was actually brown-colored contact lens. "... he was planning on passing himself off as Morgan."

"Why would he want to do that?" Josh asked as he took the lids off the remaining two boxes and set them on the bed.

"Because Richard Hensley was wanted by the FBI for murder."

Josh nodded. "Makes sense. Do you want me to take pictures of all this stuff?"

"No, just make a list of everything we find. This," I said, gesturing at the items on the bed, "is what I've come across so far."

"I'll pack it all up and take it back to the lab to inventory."

"Great. While you do that, I'll check in and around the appliances. Then once we have this stuff secured, we can flip the bed and check out the other furniture."

"Sounds like a plan," he said, shaking out one of the shirts. Then he folded it and tossed it in one of the boxes.

Leaving him to his task, I opened the fridge and grabbed the handle of the six-pack carton. After removing the beers and setting them on top of the small appliance, I peeled back every flap that had been glued into place. Finding nothing there, I placed the take-out boxes onto the counter next to the sink and, using a plastic knife I'd found on the microwave, began poking around in the larger one.

"Uh, Sarah?" Josh asked.

"Yeah." I popped open the second container and continued searching.

"Are you hungry or something?"

"No, why?"

"Well..."

When he didn't continue, I looked up and realized he'd finished loading two of the boxes, stacked them by the door, and was standing next to them, his hands on his hips, staring at me. "Then what are you doing?"

"Looking for clues."

"In a take-out box?"

"Well, yeah — maybe."

He folded his arms across his chest and tipped his head slightly to the right. "Maybe he stashed something in the air vent, or better yet, an electrical outlet. I heard spies sometimes hid important documents behind them."

"Oh come on, electrical outlets? Maybe the vent but not electrical outlets." My eyes darted around the room.

"Sarah! I was joking."

Good grief! I AM losing it! "Yeah," I said, tossing the containers into the garbage can, "I know. How about you pull out the drawers of the dresser, look on the underside of each one and then search behind them while I strip the bed. That'll make it easier to take it apart."

"What exactly am I looking for?"

"I'm not sure. At first I was looking for any kind of identification, and now we have what I can only believe is a stolen driver's license. In spite of his loyalty to Hensley, I don't think John Morgan would've just handed over his license. He told Cindy he was out of money, but I don't buy it. That's just not Richard Hensley's style. He would've had a plan of escape other than riding off on a stolen motorcycle with less than a hundred bucks in his pocket. There has to be something else here."

"Maybe he had a stash somewhere else."

"Maybe, but I doubt it. He would want to be able to keep an eye on it, so it would have to be close."

"But without him here to tell us where it is, we most likely will never find it."

"True," I said. "All we can do is make certain it's not here."

As Josh began disassembling the dresser, I folded up the top cover off the bed and put it on the small table in front of the window. I jerked off the pillowcases and stacked the pillows on top of it. Pulling the sheets off and tossing them into a pile by the door felt reminiscent of the two summers during high school I worked as a motel maid. That was when I learned the fine art of concealing things in a motel room. On two separate occasions, guests complained about a terrible odor in their room, which I was responsible for cleaning. Both had involved rotting food items; one stashed behind the drawers of the dresser and the other hidden inside the bed frame.

"Nothing here," Josh said, sliding the last drawer back into place.

"Here, let me help you and we'll check behind it." We each grabbed an end and moved the dresser away from the wall, revealing nothing but a few coins and a Do Not Disturb sign. After setting the piece of furniture back into place, we checked the underside of the fridge and microwave but again found nothing. "Last thing to check is the bed. Come on, Josh, give me a hand with the mattress."

We pulled it off and leaned it against the wall. Then we positioned ourselves, one on either side of the box spring, and lifted it up until it stood on end at the foot of the solid wood frame. "Damn it! I was sure there'd be something under here."

"Sarah," Josh began, "I think there is." He pointed toward the inside of the frame on my side. Leaning over slightly to get a better look, I spotted a small bundle of some kind, duct taped to the board. Leaving him to balance the box spring, I picked at the end of the tape until I could peel it off and the package along with it. As soon as we dropped the box spring back into place, I knelt by the bed and began tugging at the white plastic grocery bag that was wrapped around the contents. Hopelessly stuck to the tape, I finally tore the bag open, and hundred dollar bills spewed out.

"Holy cow!" Josh said, picking up the money and counting it. "There's gotta be at least ten thousand dollars here!"

"So apparently he did have money but for what?" Feeling something else in the bag, I reached in and freed an airline ticket. "This is for a United Airlines flight out of Crater Lake-Klamath Regional Airport to Portland and then connecting with a flight to Seattle. It has a departure date for next Tuesday."

"You think he was planning to hightail it north into Canada?"

"I don't know. Maybe." I handed the ticket and what was left of the bag Hensley had hidden it in to Josh. "Put this with the rest of the stuff but leave the key and the beers for Bert."

"Got it." He dropped the cash and ticket into the top box and carried all of them out to his vehicle while I flopped the mattress back into place.

"Have Cindy lock up the money when you get back," I called from the doorway of the motel room.

"Will do." He grinned. "And now you owe me two." Then he climbed in and drove away.

Certain there was nothing else to discover, I stepped out of the room and closed the door behind me. A few minutes later, I was back in front of the computer adding to my report.

I stated how I'd gained access to the room, what was found and how it was secured and removed. I did not, however, include my assumptions about how he intended to get rid of Cindy and me, nor did I include Josh's suggestion of Hensley's possible destination. After saving and printing it again, I headed for Sandusky's office.

Finding the door slightly ajar, I timidly knocked. No reply. Slowly, I pushed the door open, and when I discovered the office was empty, I took advantage of the situation. Reaching his desk in four long strides, I plopped my report right in the middle of his blotter, spun around and quickly slipped back into the hallway. Then I returned the door to its original position and left the Sheriff's Office via the rear entrance.

Chapter 26

Hey Sarah," Pete called as I stepped into the dim interior of the Silver Spur Saloon. "How's my favorite deputy?"

"Hey Pete," I replied, pushing my sunglasses up on my head and sliding onto the nearest barstool. It was still early in the world of bartending, so the place was void of customers. "I see you rode your 'baby' to work. Did you have any trouble getting it out of the Dooley?"

"No problemo." He came around the end of the bar and sat on the stool next to me. "But by the time Remy and I got back to his place and unloaded it, I didn't have time to go all the way home and switch it out for my GTO." He reached into his pocket and pulled out his extra motorcycle key and laid it on the bar. "Not taking any chances, though." We laughed, and then he stared at me for a few seconds. "So how's your day been? You look tired."

"Well you saw my morning, and it kinda went into the toilet from there."

"How's that?"

"Well, first I found out that Cindy and Sandusky are most likely going to be in a relationship. Next I stuffed myself with an unhealthy lunch."

"Yeah, I can see part of it there on your shirt," he said pointed to the faint rust-colored splotches on my uniform.

I scowled at him as I continued. "After working on my report for over an hour, I go to give it to Sandusky, and he wants to know what I found out in Hensley's motel room." I shrugged and shook my head.

"So what'd you find?"

"Some disturbing stuff but that's not the point. I didn't even think to go check it out until he mentioned it." My voice quavered and, considering it a sign of weakness, I mentally scolded myself.

"Come on Sarah," Pete soothed, pulling me closer until my head rested against his shoulder. "You've been through a helluva experience. And I'll bet you didn't get much sleep last night either, did you?" I shook my head. "So it's not surprising you're not at your best at the moment, is it?"

I pushed away from him. "But I should still be able to do my job!"

"Did you go check out the room?"

"Yes."

"And did you include what you found in your report?" I nodded. "Then you did your job. Now tell me, what did you find that was so disturbing?"

I filled him in on the map and corresponding pictures, as well as Morgan's ID, the plane ticket, and Josh's speculation.

"Makes sense."

"What doesn't make sense is the fact that I didn't recognize the man. I mean, I kept having this vague feeling of familiarity, but no way did I even consider it was Richard Hensley."

"That does seem strange. Had he really changed that much?"

"Well..." I thought about it for a second or two. "Richard was a hard-nosed FBI agent who despised facial hair and self-adornment of any kind. He wore heavy-rimmed glasses over his yellow-green eyes, and he had a paunch from drinking too much scotch. Archie Duncan was..."

"Archie Duncan was a skinny assed brown-eyed, bearded New Zealander with a snake tattoo who was hellbent on revenge. Doesn't sound to me that they were much alike. Does it to you?"

"I guess not."

"So how about it?" He stepped down from his barstool. "Are you still Deputy Sarah or just Sarah?"

I chuckled. "Just Sarah. Plain old, tired Sarah."

"Ready for that cold one I promised you?"

"Do you have any coffee?"

"You betcha. Just made it. Let me get you a cup." He went back behind the bar, grabbed an oversized white mug, and filled it with the steaming black brew. Then he added two or three packets of sugar and a huge splash of half-n-half out of the container he pulled from the fridge under the counter. "This ought to perk you up," he said, setting the hot drink in front of me.

I took a cautious sip. "Mmmm, that hits the spot. Thanks."

"That's what I like to hear." He picked up his key and re-pocketed it.

"Oh, that reminds me." I reached into my own front pocket and retrieved the items Josh had given me. "I believe these belong to you," I said, placing the key and cell phone on the bar.

"Hey, thanks." He powered up the phone. "It still works!"

"Yeah, apparently Hensley was using it to call and text Cindy. He'd even bought a charge cord for it." I savored another sip of my coffee.

"Well, glad I could oblige him — I guess." Pete said without looking up from his phone. "Uh, Sarah?"

"Yeah?"

"You said Hensley took pictures of you."

"Uh-huh."

"Where exactly?"

"In my patrol car at various locations. Why?"

He slowly rotated his phone so I could see the screen. "This is you, isn't it?" His crystal-blue eyes blazed as he passed it over.

The digital photograph was dark, having been taken in subdued lighting, yet I instantly recognized the interior of my bathhouse. "Omigod!" The pit of my stomach clenched. "He was...was right there outside my window watching me?" Anger washed over my like a tidal wave. "That son-of-a-bitch! What right did he have stalking me!" I began waving my arms wildly. "Hunting me down like an animal — trying to hurt the people I care about!"

Pete caught hold of my right wrist and retrieved his phone. "This has been through enough, don't you think?"

"Delete that picture! Delete it right now!"

"Okay, okay. Hold on." He pushed a couple of buttons and then set the phone on the bar. "There, all gone."

I glared at him for a few seconds and then shook my head. "Sorry, sorry. It all just makes me so, so..." That was it. My fatigue, after being tossed about on a rollercoaster of emotions, hit rock bottom. Burying my face in my hands, giant sobs rocked my body. Suddenly Pete was beside me, his strong arms wrapped around me and holding me tightly.

"No problemo," he whispered, his mouth nuzzled against my ear. Slowly the sobs subsided, as I relaxed into his embrace. Too relaxed apparently as neither of us heard the front door open until it was too late.

"Young woman, arrest that man!" a female voice ordered.

Marjorie Callaghan!

Pete jumped back as I leapt from the stool and spun around. I'd recognized the voice but not the short-statured woman before me. Dressed in a pink business suit, her steel gray hair was free from its bun and secured by a large wooden barrette at the nape of her neck.

"Why should I arrest Pete?" I asked.

"The motorcycle that nearly ran me off the road is parked outside, and since he's the only other person in here, it must be his."

"Yes it belongs to him, but I can assure you he's not the one who ran you off the road."

"Is that so?" She placed her hands on her hips.

"That's right, ma'am," Pete offered, stepping toward her. "You see it was stolen, and it's the thief you met on the road."

"Well I hope that maniac is in custody."

"No ma'am," I said. "He's dead."

Marjorie's eyes widened. "That seems a bit harsh for stealing and wreckless driving, don't you think."

"How about for kidnapping and attempted

221

murder?" The words were out of my mouth before I could stop them.

"Kidnapping? Murder?" She marched over to the bar and climbed onto the stool next to where I'd been sitting. "Did you shoot him?"

Shaking my head, I reclaimed my seat and Pete slipped back behind the bar. "No Marjorie, the snake killed him," I said, wondering if she'd mind the un-invited familiarity.

She didn't. "I see." She stared straight ahead.

I glanced at Pete and saw his mustache twitch as he tried not to laugh. "You can read about it in next week's paper," I said.

"Would you like a cup of coffee, Ms. Callaghan?" Pete asked.

"Don't much care for coffee, young man."

"Please, call me Pete. Can I get you something else?"

"Well... I wouldn't mind a shot of Yukon Jack. That is, if the deputy here isn't going to arrest me for drinking and driving."

Pete's mustache twitched again. "You're in luck," he said. "She's off-duty."

Marjorie looked at me, and I shrugged. "Well, what are you waiting for?" she demanded.

"Coming right up." Pete filled a shot glass with the slightly sweet, amber-colored liquor, and placed it in front of the woman.

She took a small sip, savoring it before swallow-ing. Raising the glass to her lips again, she downed the rest of the liquor in one gulp, slammed the emp-ty shot glass upside down on the bar, and wiped her mouth on the back of her hand. "Delicious!" Then she slid from her perch and left without saying another word.

Pete and I looked at each other and burst into laughter. "If I hadn't seen that with my own eyes..." he began.

"I wouldn't have believed it either." I stood and stretched. "Well, I'm going to head home."

Pete walked me toward the door. "You gonna be all right?" he asked, wrapping his arm around my shoulders. "I can get Shellie to cover for me if you want some company."

"Thanks, but I'll be fine. Probably just go home and sleep for two days."

He gave me a big hug. "Call me if you change your mind."

"Will do." Then I left the Spur and headed for Remy's.

Chapter 27

Unlike most of my trips back and forth on County Road 1 in the last couple of weeks, my drive north was more leisurely and by the time I reached Fort Bidwell, it was almost five o'clock. I pulled into Remy's driveway, shut off the engine, and sat in my unit watching Bubbles and Millie chase each other across the yard. *So tired!* I closed my eyes and let my mind drift. But before it could drift too far, I was startled by a rap on my window.

Opening my eyes, I was greeted by an elderly man wearing a black felt hat. "Hi Remy," I said as I climbed out. "How was your day?"

"Busy, busy. Had lots of chores to do, but I got them all done. How did the rest of your day turn out?"

"Don't ask because I don't want to talk about it. At least not now." I undid my gun belt and tucked it under my seat.

"Fair enough." He started for the house. "Why don't you come on around back and set a spell on the porch? Got some cold beer in the refrigerator."

I followed him as far as the front steps. "Thanks but I think I'll take a rain check. I'm exhausted and could really use a shower."

"You hungry? I could wrestle you up something if you are."

"Not right now. Mostly I just want to sleep."

"Sure, sure. I'll round up the mutt for you." He pulled in his lower lip and let out a shrill whistle. Within seconds, the two animals in Remy's care came bounding around the house and tumbled into a heap at his feet. I reached down and retrieved the small dog that lived with me.

"Thanks Remy," I said, as I turned to walk back to the Explorer.

"Hold up a second and let me get your key." He hurried up the steps and through the front door.

Key? What key? I still hadn't figured out what he was talking about until he returned and placed a Ford ignition key in my hand. "The Dooley!"

"What in tarnation did you think I was giving you?"

"To be honest, I had no idea."

He shook his head. "Girl, you better go straight to bed and stay there."

"I will." I started toward the Explorer again. "And thanks for taking my truck home for me."

"Oh it was no trouble. Me and the critters had a nice walk back."

I had to chuckle. Only Remy would load up a goat and a small dog to drive a vehicle five hundred yards. I thanked Remy again and drove home.

After swapping out my uniform for just a pair of cutoff sweats and my Green Bay T-shirt, I wandered into the kitchen to see if I had any cold beers of my own. As I moved past the kitchen table, I noticed a hand-written note and what appeared to be a bullet slug. My heart leapt into my throat. *Now what?*

Cautiously I picked up the note and slowly read it aloud. "I'm no forensic investigator, but I'm pretty sure you killed an innocent bag of flour. I found this slug amongst what was left of the bag. Anyway, got the mess cleaned up for you. Figured you'd turn down dinner, so there's a casserole in the oven. Get some rest, Partner."

Laughing, I peered into the pantry. The entire mess was gone. Every pot and pan must have been washed and the shelves scrubbed down. *Unbelievable!* Then I opened the oven. The aroma of cheesy tomato sauce filled my nostrils and made my stomach growl. Remy had definitely been busy today.

Checking in the fridge, I spotted two lonely beers on the top shelf. I grabbed them and my cell phone, and Bubbles and I went outside to find a comfortable spot where I could call Sue back. Settled into the Adirondack chair under the apple tree, I opened one of the beers and took a couple of swallows. Then I propped both legs up onto one of its arms and punched in Sue's number.

"Hey, Sarah."

"Hi, Sue."

"How you doin'?"

"I'm okay. Tired but okay. Listen Sue, I may have some information, but I need to ask you a question first."

"Okay, shoot."

"Do you know if John Morgan ever said anything about losing or missing his driver's license around the time of Hensley's dismissal?"

"Yeah, he did. How did you know?"

For the second time that day, I described what I'd found, omitting the photos on Pete's phone, and my speculations of Hensley's plans. "There might be a complication, though," I told Sue when I'd finished. "I'm not certain Sandusky is going to notify the FBI about Hensley.

She laughed. "I don't think that will be a problem. The deputy director is flying out there personally to take charge of the situation. Something about him wanting to make damn sure it was Hensley."

"As much as I would like to see that, I'm glad I have the next two days off," I confessed.

Sue laughed again. "Now that you're not being pursued by a friggin' lunatic, I've got something to ask you?"

"What's that?"

"How's your love life?"

Good grief! "I have been pretty busy, you know. Recovering stolen Indian artifacts..."

"Native American," she corrected.

"Sorry, Native American artifacts, solving murders, recovering bodies. The list goes on and on."

"Cut the crap, Sarah. You seeing anyone or not?"

Good old Sue, always straight to the point. "Well..." I hesitated for dramatic effect.

"Well, what? Spill it!"

It was working. "Sort of."

"How do you sort of see someone?"

"I drove him and his motorcycle to a race in the Nevada desert, and we went for drinks and dinner with some friends in Alturas." I left out the part about him tagging along with Remy to rescue me.

"What's his name? Is he cute? What's he do?"

"Whoa, slow down!" I could practically hear her jumping up and down. "His name is Pete, he owns a local bar, and we are just friends."

"Friends, huh? Well at least that's a start."

Yes, I had to agree; it was a start. "Look Sue, I gotta go. I'm exhausted and need to go to bed."

"Alone?"

Gimme a break. "Yes, alone."

She howled with laughter. "All right then, girl-friend. Stay in touch."

I snapped my phone shut and polished off my beer. I thought about crawling into bed but decided a soak in the hot tub sounded better. "Come on, Bubbles. Wanna go for a swim?" The small dog got up from his spot near my chair and shook out his ungroomed coat. Other than size, he looked nothing like the prissy dog my sister had sent to stay with me.

I stepped into the bathhouse, put my phone and unopened beer on the windowsill, and turned on the hose. While the water from the geothermal spring filled the tub, I strolled toward the field where Raven was quietly grazing. Just before I reached the gate, I stopped and told Bubbles to sit. As with every time before, his haunches hit the ground.

Reaching the fence, I whistled. The black horse raised his head, ears forward, and whinnied. Then he trotted over to where I was waiting, hung his huge head over the fence and nudged me. "Hey big fella," I said as I scratched his flat forehead and rubbed his ears. "Have I missed you." The horse nudged me again. "I know I haven't spent much time with you." I scratched the base of his mane. "I promise we'll go on more adventures. You know, like the day we ran into Pete by Fee Reservoir. That was fun wasn't it?"

He moved his velvet nose up and down, and I had to chuckle. There were times when I truly thought the animal understood every word I said. "And then there's Pete." Raven nudged me again. "Oh quit pushing. You're as bad as Sue." Then I hugged his massive neck and headed to the bathhouse. Looking back over my shoulder, I was surprised to see Bubbles still sitting where I'd left him. "Well come on, Dog. Let's go." He trotted toward me, tongue hanging and tail wagging, and we went inside the small building.

The water had almost reached the top and was deliciously warm. I shut off the hose and twisted off the cap of my last beer. Sitting on the edge of the tub, I dangled my feet in the water and sipped my beer. When most of it was gone, I set it back on the sill, pulled off my clothes and slipped into the water. As I sank to the bottom caressed by the soothing mineral-laden water, all the tension that had been building in my neck and shoulders over the last few days faded away.

When I floated back up to the surface of the water, I was greeted by the shaggy grin of a miniature mutt. "Hanging out with Remy has certainly improved your manners. Do you want to get in?" Bubbles stood and wagged his tail. "Well get in here, then." The dog leapt into the tub right in front of me and began paddling around.

"Pace yourself," I warned. "I don't plan on getting out until I'm good and pruny."

"He really is a beautiful animal," Shellie said as the four of us strolled from the pasture back toward the house. "So majestic!"

I laughed. "I always considered Raven more of a pesky troublemaker."

"Now hold on there," Remy interjected. "That

there horse saved my bacon not so long ago, so I won't have you badmouthin' him none."

"Okay Remy, I'm sorry." I smiled at the neighbor who had saved my own bacon a couple of times himself.

He nodded his approval. "What I want to know is where did you learn to make such goldarn delicious ribs. Thought you were more of a heat-n-serve kinda gal."

"Glad you liked them." I glanced over at Pete. "I had a little help from a southern bartender with a secret family recipe."

"Well, the two of you can rustle up those any time you like."

"I agree," Shellie added. "They were so delicious I ate more than I should have."

"Hope you saved room for apple pie," Remy said.

"I did," I assured him. The first time he'd brought one of his apple pies to my house was the day we met. It was so good, I'd eaten the whole thing, minus the one piece he'd had, in less than twenty-four hours.

"I'm sure I can manage a slice," Pete said, patting his stomach.

Shellie laughed. "But no pressure, right?"

"I just don't want it going to..." Something in the distance attracted Remy's attention. "What in tarnation is that?" he asked, pointing to where the road dropped down from the top of the ridge just past his place. A black limousine coasted down the small incline, slowing as it approached my driveway, and pulled in.

"You expecting anybody?" Pete asked as we all watched it ease toward the house.

"No, can't say that I am," I replied. "Unless..."

The long automobile slowed to a stop a few feet away, and the driver got out and hustled around to the passenger door.

"Unless what?" Pete asked.

A tall, thin man with dark hair and a goatee and a woman with short blond hair dressed in a sleeveless red dress climbed out and started around the vehicle. I didn't recognize him, but was certain the woman was —

"Sarah, darling," she called, her wave cut short as she attempted to negotiate the gravel driveway in red stilettos.

Alexis!

"Come on, time to go." Remy let out a shrill whistle, and the two tiny playmates who had been frolicking around the yard came scampering over. He scooped up the goat and started down my driveway.

"Remy, where are you going?" Shellie asked, chasing after him.

"Home."

"What about the pie?"

"Not to worry," he called over his shoulder, "I made two of them."

"But..." She looked back at us and shrugged her shoulders.

"It's okay," I said, waving her on. "I'll explain later."

"All right. Thanks for having us over," she said. "I've enjoyed our get-togethers the past couple of weeks. Hope we can do it some more." Then she headed after Remy, who had almost reached the road.

"How are you?" My sister, along with her traveling

companion, had finally made it close enough to give me a hug.

"I'm fine, Alexis. How are you?"

"C'est magnifique!" she said. "Sterling and I had a wonderful time, didn't we dear?" She looped her arm through his.

"Certainement, ma chère."

Oh brother! I looked at Pete and rolled my eyes. "Pleased to meet you," I said, holding my hand out to Sterling. "This is my friend, Pete." The men shook hands. "Pete, this is my sister, Alexis."

"Hello," he said, touching the brim of an invisible hat.

She flashed him her million-dollar smile. "Say," she said, leaning toward me, "wasn't that your nasty neighbor that just left?"

I scowled at her. "Yes, that was Remy."

"So where's my precious baby?" She looked around and then called, "Bubbles."

After having his playmate hauled off, the dog had moseyed over to his favorite spot under the apple tree. When he heard his name, he got to his feet and trotted over.

"Oh look," Alexis said. "Is that your dog, Pete?"

"No ma'am," he replied.

"Actually," I bent down and picked up the miniature mutt, "it's your dog."

My sister stared at me for at least half a minute. "That scruffy-looking mongrel," she said, pointing at Bubbles, "is my precious baby girl?"

"Well, yes and no," I said. "It's your baby but not a girl."

Alexis placed her hands on her hips. "What are you talking about?"

"Well, I couldn't get all the stickers out with the scissors, so I had to shave the belly and around the back legs and I discovered that — here, let me show you." I turned Bubbles around and held up his backend for inspection. "See, he has balls."

"Ewwwww!!" Alexis exclaimed, frantically waving her hands. "Put him down, put him down."

"Oh come on, it's the same dog." I lowered Bubbles, rotated him and tucked him under my right arm like a football. "You'll just need to dress him differently."

"Well..." She looked at Sterling, who remained strangely quiet. "I have seen some awfully cute things for boy dogs. Maybe I can swing a swap with her, I mean his, old clothes."

"That might be a problem," I said.

"Oh?" She pursed her lips as she raised her eyebrows.

"They kind of got chewed up."

"You let the dog chew up the clothes. Why?"

"I didn't exactly let him do it. I had to go on a call and forgot he was all alone in the house. By the time I got back, it was too late. He'd chewed up the clothes as well as the trunk they were in."

"The trunk! I loved that trunk."

"I'm sure you did. I'm sorry."

"Well, I suppose I can find one that's not so girly." She held out her hands. "Come to Mommy, Bubbles. Time to go home."

The small dog in my arms sniffed at my sister a couple of times and let at a low guttural growl.

She snatched her hands back. "What's the matter with her, I mean him?"

I shook my head. "I don't know. Maybe he's just

nervous. Here." I stepped closer to Alexis and placed the dog in her arms. The growling increased in volume and intensity.

"Take him, take him," Alexis shrieked, practically tossing the dog at me.

"I don't get it," I said. "He's never done that before." I returned Bubbles to the football hold and scratched the top of his head. The growling immediately ceased.

"Looks like he prefers his Aunt Sarah," Pete offered.

"But he's Alexis' dog, not mine. He needs to go home with her." I held the dog out to her and again he began to growl.

"Oh Sterling," she sobbed, clinging to her companion, "my baby doesn't love me anymore."

"I'm sure that if we put him in the crate you sent him in, he will calm down by the time you get home." I handed Bubbles to Pete. "I'll go get it."

"No Sarah, wait." My sister dabbed her eyes with a white linen handkerchief Sterling had suddenly produced. "It's obvious Bubbles likes you better than me, so I'm giving her, I mean him, to you. Come on Sterling, we're leaving." Without another word, the two of them climbed back into the limo. The driver fired up its engine and backed it toward Raven's field until he could maneuver it onto the driveway.

"Why didn't you try to stop her?" Pete asked as we watched the limousine climb the small hill and vanish from sight.

I plucked Bubbles from his arms. "I'm not sure. Maybe I didn't want him to have to wear those ridiculous clothes anymore." I set him down on the ground, and he proceeded to run around us and bark. "Maybe I wasn't ready to give him up just yet."

Pete wrapped his arm around my waist. "I think he wasn't ready to give you up, either."

I smiled. "Maybe not. We do kinda make a good team. Maybe I'll make him a full-time partner and take him on patrol."

"Better not let Remy hear you call him that," Pete teased. "Now how about some of that apple pie?"

"Sounds good. And if you want to stick around for a while, maybe we can find something worth watching on television."

"Are you asking me to spend the night?"

"Maybe." I grinned at him. "Maybe not."